"The kiss…?" Jesse wound the towel in his hand. Worry creased his brow.

"I'd say it was a 9.25."

"Huh!"

She explained in a lighthearted tone, "Technique was good—"

"Good?" He shook his head. "You were moaning as soon as our lips touched. That's more than good."

"Fine. Excellent. Delivery exceptional. Follow-through… didn't really maximize."

"Not my fault. You were the hungry one."

"And no follow-up. No information on what to do for a repeat performance." Belinda licked her lips. Even though she teased, she did expect him to play to his bad-boy image. Instead, he was the perfect gentleman.

"Well…I'll take that under advisement." He paused as if considering the situation. "I didn't want to have to hope that you wouldn't kick me off the job."

She shook her head. Obviously, their tentative approaches dampened the impulse to go after what they both had felt. Well, she didn't need a do-over. Simply a continuation would suffice.

Dear Reader,

I hope all is well with you and yours. I've had a wonderful time digging further into the Meadows family and discovering the strength and pride that infuses this family. Cousins can be as close as blood sisters, maybe even to enjoy better relationships.

One to Love is the continuation of the celebration of family. I believe that we all need a supportive group of individuals as we journey through life. People who will love and counsel us. As we receive those gifts and blessings, we should share those gifts with others.

Think about those positive sisterly bonds that have given you strength and shaped you into the person you are and will continue to become. Now, pick up the phone and give that person(s) a call, jump in your car and go visit, or book a flight and go celebrate. Tomorrow isn't promised.

Live life to the fullest.

Peace,

Michelle

ONE to Love

MICHELLE MONKOU

HARLEQUIN® KIMANI™ ROMANCE

Recycling programs
for this product may
not exist in your area.

ISBN-13: 978-0-373-86400-3

One to Love

Copyright © 2015 by Michelle Monkou

HARLEQUIN®
™ www.Harlequin.com

Printed in U.S.A.

Michelle Monkou became a world traveler at the age of three, when she left her birthplace of London, England, and moved to Guyana, South America. She then moved to the US as a young teen. Michelle was nominated for the 2003 Emma Award for Favorite New Author, and she continues to write romances with complex characters and intricate plots.

Visit her website for further information at michellemonkou.com, or contact her at michellemonkou@comcast.net.

Books by Michelle Monkou

Harlequin Kimani Romance

Sweet Surrender
Here and Now
Straight to the Heart
No One But You
Gamble on Love
Only in Paradise
Trail of Kisses
The Millionaire's Ultimate Catch
If I Had You
Racing Hearts
Passionate Game
One of a Kind
One to Love

Visit the Author Profile page at Harlequin.com for more titles

To sisters everywhere and to those who may not share the genes, but still share those bonds.

Chapter 1

"One more, Jesse. Come on. Concentrate!"

Jesse gritted his teeth, grabbed the handgrips and grunted out five more leg presses. After the last push, he swore into the exhalation. Pain from no single source exploded throughout his legs. His back ached, as if wanting in on the torture. He stayed put in the chair until he trusted his legs to hold him upright. Sweat bathed his face and body like a second skin. With the sweep of his arm, he wiped his face dry. It didn't really help when his skin sprouted another layer of perspiration.

"Good. You did good." Olivier, his trainer, clapped his shoulder.

Jesse nodded. He kept his doubt to himself. Recovering from a cracked pelvis and lower back injury felt like scaling a sheer rock face with his legs tied.

The last thing he wanted this morning was a chipper lecture about his future. Finally, he stood and extricated himself from the machine. A groan of bitter frustration escaped. "Thanks for coming to my side of the world."

"Yeah, well, three days with you are more than enough. I'll be heading back to Madrid tomorrow. Scouts are presenting their reports to management. Otherwise, I'd stick around to make your life miserable. Make sure you're keeping up with your strength exercises."

Jesse nodded. "Don't worry. They work me hard here. Not quite at your kick-butt level, but they don't mind seeing me walking, instead of crawling, out of the gym." He hated to see his friend leave. It was good to see a familiar face, even if Olivier didn't let up one inch on the workout.

"I'm hoping that you'd changed your mind." The older man didn't bother to look up from his task. He sprayed the length of the seat and handgrips with antibacterial cleanser and wiped off the surfaces.

"You and everyone else." Jesse shook his head. "Can't deal with any pressure right now."

"Can't or won't?"

"It's not a debate."

"You're right." Olivier held up his hands in surrender. His tone softened. "Take your time. Then come back better than new."

Jesse didn't respond. The last time he opened his mouth about his future, he'd announced his retirement from professional soccer at twenty-nine years old. Walking away from the game had sent an earthquake-size ripple through the league. The frenzied media still stirred like rabid dogs at any possibility of his comeback, although he had barely six months of physical therapy under his belt. On everyone's breath was his place on next year's World Cup team.

"We all care about you."

Jesse shrugged, which was his favorite gesture to get anyone off his back.

Olivier motioned toward the exercise mat. Time for the dreaded stretches. Another fifteen minutes of agony. "Ease into it." His trainer gently coaxed Jesse to hold the position until his stubborn muscles improved their range of motion.

If the pain and stiffness could be colors, the torture would be dark bloodred and stark winter white. That's what he saw with his eyes squeezed shut, jaws clenched, while he was concentrating on not shouting out in pain.

Screaming or cussing, either option didn't matter. Both had their place in his recovery. Bad luck had screwed him royally with a freak collision by a defender as he gunned it to the goal. For his trouble, the human bulldozer scooped him up, carried him for several feet and dumped him facedown with a crushing cleat imprint on his hip for good measure.

Most didn't have to experience a body-numbing injury. Its suddenness felt like the quick snap of a light switch. Nor did most have to deal with panic that rushed through the body with the power of a flash flood. In its wake were thick layers of fear—could he walk? Could he finish the game? When his gaze had slid away from the concerned faces, and their voices had faded, he stared upward at the sky in all its brightness with one pressing thought—his career was over.

After the surgery, his fears continued to press on him, but they were his to keep, deal with and to hide from prying minds of the analysts, his agent, the team and those behind the moneymaking decisions. It was better for him to toss out retirement as an option before they tossed him aside in a trade or to a lower division, for not meeting expectations of his contract. Although his body shifted into high gear with its healing, Jesse still didn't retract comments about his retirement. Something held him back.

"Have you been following up with the doctors?" Olivier turned attention to the other side of Jesse's body.

"They recommend another round of surgery, depending on how well I complete the physical," Jesse shared.

"You're sounding doubtful, son."

Jesse shrugged. "All the tinkering is not going to put me back together again."

"You don't know that. Leave it to the experts."

"That's just the thing. I'm tired of the experts."

"You'll be one hundred percent. With the physical rehab, you'll be the powerhouse that you are."

"Were."

Olivier's frown ascended his face and settled in the narrow space between his thick eyebrows. "Cut the pity party, Jesse. You were known as a raging bull on that field. Players saw you coming and hoped they'd live to see another day. You can maneuver a path to the goal with the precision of a shark. It's what you were born to do."

"Now you sound like my father." Jesse pushed Olivier's hand away from his sore hip. Not that he was in extreme pain, but the site of his shattered bones was his personal demon that haunted him. He could barely look at the long scars, much less touch them.

"Talk to someone. Get the anger out. It's easy for your thoughts to be scrambled. That was a major shake-up."

"So now you want me to talk to a shrink. I know what I want…"

"To quit? Walk away? I'm not accepting your retirement. No one is, actually." Olivier stood over him, open frustration evident in his thin lips clenched together. "You have enough time to get ready for the World Cup."

"World Cup?" Jesse snorted. If this was any other moment, he would spring to his feet and walk away. "I'm done. I'm not having second thoughts. And now with soccer out of my life, I've got nothing to show for it."

"You have money, trophies. Fans adore you. Women want to…"

"Enough." Jesse wanted no reminders about his carefree, have-it-all mentality. Only supermodels and hot, sexy A-list actresses interested him. *Used to.* They never lasted long enough as his girlfriend to cause drama. His blunt attitude nipped that in the bud, but did little to shake off the determined ones.

Flashbacks of his behavior sickened him. A lot of things sickened him. Anger and sadness rotated their position in his head and heart. Recuperating for weeks in a body cast had drawn back the blinds and let the brutal reality shine in because, straight up, no one—sportscasters, any talking head expert on the sport, and fantasy-soccer aficionados—gave a damn about him now.

"You're down, but temporarily. I get how frustrating it all feels. I've been working with athletes for twenty years. Trust me. This will pass." Olivier lowered his hand to help him. The thick, bushy eyebrows twitched over his eyes, which regarded his client piercingly.

Jesse wanted to slap away the hand. He didn't want any help. Or pity. Or comfort. He wanted to be alone without his usual flashy trappings. But even that, he couldn't do. With nowhere else to retreat, he'd stepped back in time with his return to his hometown. At the end of the day, all he had was family. His parents were willing to offer him more than a helping hand, while he rehabilitated. They offered sanctuary until the speculation about his injury died down a bit. The supportive shoulder wasn't quite his brother's— Diego's—style. Well, Mr. Ivy League could get in line with those who gloated over soccer's "show pony" hitting rock bottom—a six-month tumultuous downward slide.

"Are we good?"

"Yeah." Jesse swallowed his pride and allowed himself to be hoisted to his feet. He couldn't be angry with Olivier. The man had become more like a substitute father and mentor when Jesse first crossed the hallowed ground of soccer by becoming a professional player with the youth soccer academy at seventeen years old.

They shook hands and parted ways in the parking lot. Olivier would return to the management of the Spanish team with no headway to report. And Jesse would get in his car to head home and soak his over-worked body in the tub. Nursing a bottle of beer, he could tune out nagging doubts about his future.

Hours later, instead of grabbing another drink, Jesse tossed back two pain relievers and gulped down a glass of water. Sleep eluded him. And he was in no mood to chase after it. Rather than head for his bed, he walked out onto the deck of his houseboat and flopped into his favorite lounge chair.

The early spring season had just enough of a warm edge for him to enjoy being on the deck. Without the harsh lights from street lamps, the brilliance of the stars stood out against the inky dark sky. Star-gazing was the perfect cure for his restless thoughts. Out here, he didn't have to worry about annoying re-porters. The marina had solid security and so far the sports journalists didn't know about his temporary residence. Unfortunately, they tended to stake their reporting platforms near his parents' home.

His cell phone rang. Probably his mother or father. He answered for the usual nightly check-in.

"Where were you tonight?" This wasn't his mom or dad.

"Diego?" Jesse didn't expect to hear his younger brother's voice. "What are you talking about?"

"We were expecting you for dinner. Mom and Dad had the Tompkins family over to meet you."

Jesse swore. He'd forgotten. After the workout and the conversation with Olivier, quiet and solitude were all he craved for the remainder of the day. His parents had set up a steady stream of brunches and dinners with him trotting, or rather limping, in to meet church members, coworkers and his mother's crochet—or was it cross-stitch?—group. After these past several weeks of smiling, signing autographs and posing for photos, he'd come to dread the invitations. Instead of saying anything, he'd come up with excuses not to attend, arrive super late or be stoic and unresponsive to occasional flirtations. But this was the first time that he'd completely wiped it from his mind.

"And they brought their kids."

Jesse squeezed his eyes shut. "I didn't know kids were coming."

"Is that all you have to say?" Diego pushed.

"I'll make my apologies to Mom. Is she around?" Jesse didn't want to get into anything with his brother. Not tonight. They could fight tomorrow or the day after when there was no threat of them running out of things to irritate each other.

Apparently, Diego didn't want to let up. "This was a waste of my time, too."

"I didn't ask you to attend. Never did." Jesse rubbed the length of his thigh. His mood turned sour.

"No, you didn't ask, but still I came. Mom expected us to be there."

"And you're not one to disappoint." Jesse stared out into the night.

No longer focused on the stars, he looked out at the lakeside houses' lights dotting either shore. His temper brewed. Friction that had been in the making for most of their lives bubbled like a volcano. Their disagreements waxed and waned, depending on their parents' involvement to push a peace process. While his busy soccer schedule and obligations once provided a safe zone, lately signs warned that the turbulence was on the rise, a change that he'd noticed when he returned home for his indefinite stay.

Jesse continued, "Tell Mom that I'll call her in the morning." No matter how much he'd rather not have to meet his parents' friends, he never wanted to disappoint kids if he could help it. They mattered, especially with their unconditional loyalty and support. He had hundreds of letters since his injury to prove his point.

Tomorrow, he'd be on it. If he had to go to the Tompkins' home and take the kids for an ice cream treat, he'd make the experience fun with selfies and autographs.

But Diego didn't let up. "Sure thing. There's always an event or woman that is more important. Let me remind you that the false love and adoration won't last. Because, then what happens now that the soccer god is shown to be human?"

Jesse didn't reply. He didn't have to respond since Diego abruptly ended the call. His brother's challenge had echoes of truth, though.

His thigh throbbed—a final punishment for the night. He leaned back his head and closed his eyes to will away the ache.

Anger was all he mustered up for himself. Disappointment was all he seemed to stir from others. So why on earth had he felt compelled to come back to the city of Midway, New York?

Three months later

Belinda Toussaint had barely nestled her butt onto her office chair for the morning when Tawny, her assistant, hovered in the doorway. At least she came with a proffered mug of coffee. Steam curled enticingly upward from the hot elixir. The robust scent magically jolted her brain awake.

"I've got good news." Tawny held her position in the doorway, only extending the hand that held the coffee, a gift from the gods. "And I've got bad news."

Was the mug with the words *Professional Badass* supposed to energize her for the good news? Or stroke her ego for the bad news?

Belinda beckoned Tawny to come closer. She relieved her assistant of the offering. "Thanks." She took a careful sip, letting it wash over her tongue, before closing her eyes with a grateful sigh. "Okay, what now? Lay down the yucky stuff. This Wednesday is starting on the wrong side of my emotions."

"Mail already arrived." Tawny raised the cluster of envelopes clutched in her other hand. Today, the fingernails were painted bright periwinkle blue. Her burgundy-dyed hair was styled in spiral curls. Bright eyes blinked out at her behind black-framed glasses.

What Belinda noted more, however, was that Tawny didn't hand over any of the mail. "Are those bills?"

Tawny shook her head. "It's worse." She scrunched her nose.

"Worse than having to pay out money?" As far as Belinda was concerned, things couldn't get much worse than starting a new business, specifically a nonprofit.

Mentally, she ticked off what she could tout as a new owner. One employee—Tawny. No real clients to speak of…yet. In this one-room converted barn-turned-office, they shared the work space and had carved out a storage area. Belinda framed her office with thin drywall and equipped it with a salvaged door that was more for aesthetics than for privacy. Other than her desk and two chairs, a single column of file drawers that hopefully soon would contain a large number of clients' information filled a corner in her office. A small clay pot with a thriving ivy plant draped the top.

"Got a response about my complaint." Tawny's mouth pursed. "The secondhand store where we bought these so-called antiques won't give us back our money. Stuff wasn't even fit for a yard sale."

"At least we were able to decorate the welcome room. And part of the donation went to a good cause." Belinda wasn't surprised. The hodgepodge furniture selection was from one of the large thrift stores in the city.

"Please. You need to check to see if the soup kitchen did get any of that money. Those people saw an easygoing, prone-to-guilt woman. And they got paid. Next time, don't buy anything based on online pictures."

Belinda waved off Tawny's constant dig that, when it came to her business, she should stop giving her heart and soul. That she needed to toughen up. It was funny how the advice sounded similar to what she'd said to Dana, her youngest cousin, who now ran the family media empire.

Tawny cleared her throat. "Not done."

"Okay, bring on the bad news. In an hour, we have a prospective client coming in to see the facility and get more information. I want to make sure that she's blown away with the work in progress. More important that she's willing to sign up."

"Once we start, those good reviews will roll in, and we'll be busier than you could've ever imagined." Tawny flopped into the only chair. She pulled out the letter and unfolded it. "From the *Brandywine Gazette*, 'Dear Mrs. Belinda Toussaint—'"

"Good grief. I'm not married. I'm thirty and single. They're giving me bad news *and* don't give a damn to address me correctly."

"'We have enjoyed being a part of building the Dreamweaver Riding Program. Your dedication to assisting young people to overcome challenges with equine-assisted therapy solutions is admirable. We treasure this opportunity beyond measure.'"

"Get on with it," Belinda prompted. Her fingers on one hand restlessly chipped away the ragged polish on her other hand.

"'Due to budgetary constraints, we are unable to continue to be part of the sponsorship program. We look forward to working with you in the future. Good luck with your endeavors.'"

"You could've paraphrased all of that into *we're screwed*." Belinda leaned back in her chair and swiveled around to face the wall that held her vision board for the riding program.

Her ideas, from small thoughts to grand dreams, covered the wall in the form of pinned drawings and pictures. In a separate space, a timeline displayed the renovations for the stable and riding ring and arrival dates of three additional horses, along with the training and rehabilitation equipment. In big, bold letters, the launch date mocked her goal to have a facility to open in three months.

This massive undertaking hadn't been a smooth one. Many times, she'd had to adjust the timeline. Once she'd suffered a major meltdown and wanted to quit. Her cousins Fiona and Dana had rallied around her until her fears had retreated, somewhat. Their push was enough to get her mind back firmly on the goal.

At the start, this riding-therapy program would cater to children and teens experiencing physical, cognitive and even emotional stresses and disabilities. Success rested with using the right-tempered horses in the program. The animals had been documented to successfully help with patients' physical and emotional challenges. Moreover, the beasts' gentle natures coaxed children to emerge from behind their shells of shyness or low self-esteem, to learn to trust in their own abilities and to show them, through caring for the horses, how to develop connections outside of their comfort zones, with others. Eventually, her program would expand its services to include adults, especially war veterans, a need that she'd realized recently after completing research.

Right now, she had a small number of clients who used her horses for their once-a-week or weekend rides. However, regardless of her best intentions, it took money to run the operation. Where insurance or income couldn't pay the fee, she expected donations would fill the gap. Starting at the beginning of this year, under the Dreamweaver logo, she'd held a small number of fund-raisers, strategic PR advertising and networking events that had netted a handful of donors and their financial pledges. Of course, there was more money in the flashier charities. Donors with the deep pockets preferred the major publicity that came as a result of their newsworthy gifts. All she could offer was a sincere thank-you, a glowing write-up in the local newspaper that no longer would be a donor, and a heavy piece of crystal with their name etched for all posterity to see.

She turned back to her desk, reached for the chewable antacids and waited for them to take effect.

"Don't worry, Belinda. It will happen. What you're doing is a really good thing."

"Yeah, but sometimes good isn't good enough." The current operations cost a fortune. Her plans to expand would take her expenses over the edge. Chasing donations wasn't her shtick. Tawny was a good organizer and cheerleader, but she hadn't shown any prowess for prying dollars out of prospective donors, either. And that wasn't why she had been hired. Dana had helped provide part-time volunteers for fund-raising, but it was time to have a full-time person on staff solely dedicated to fund-raising. An added expense to the profit and loss statement. She sighed.

Tawny held up her hand. "More news."

"We're still on the bad stuff, right?"

Her assistant nodded. "But not as bad. It's a tweak and could work out to be better. I think—"

"Oh, for heaven's sake, get on with it." Belinda rubbed her forehead and waited for the next drop of the hammer.

"Ed Santiago, your contractor, called a few minutes ago. Actually, his wife. Ed is on bed rest. Angina."

"Oh, no. Should he be home? He shouldn't mess around with heart issues."

"He's got to follow up with his doctor. For now, he's home and they've adjusted his pressure meds."

"I'm glad that it wasn't worse." Belinda didn't want to think of the dire possibilities.

"Not to worry, though. He's sending his son Jesse to finish managing the renovations."

Belinda waved off the additional news. "I'm going to send him flowers."

Tawny nodded. "I pulled up a couple arrangements on my computer. Pick the one you like and I'll have the order there by tomorrow."

"Thanks." Belinda hated to hear about the nose-dive Ed's health had taken. The man wasn't exactly at the youthful end of the age spectrum, but he was active and a conscientious worker. She couldn't help but feel uneasy with his unexpected absence. Well, she felt more guilt than unease because the clock on the project ticked loudly.

"Jesse will be arriving soon to meet you and go over the remainder of the schedule."

"I don't want this…Jesse. I've never met him. There's no way that he can replace Ed's expertise. There's no time for someone new to come in and putz around."

"This isn't just a regular person. It's Jesse Santiago."

Belinda shrugged and shook her head. "And?"

"Football star."

"I don't need a quarterback here."

"No. I mean soccer. He's a soccer superstar, really."

"Calm down with the giddy smile. We don't need

a sports jock." Belinda's fingers had managed to clear the red nail polish completely off two fingernails.

Tawny rolled her eyes. "That term is so '80s. Because I've heard of Jesse and his mad skills, I did research." She placed a one-page printout on the desk that had a small photo image in the right corner of the page. With her blue-painted nail, she slid a finger over the information.

"A résumé?" Belinda didn't bother picking up the paper. She really wasn't interested in whatever the internet had captured, unless he had a mug shot or arrest record. Tawny's nail-tapping for her attention finally motivated her to act interested. She picked up the page and scanned the details.

Jesse Santiago was a former professional soccer player for Madrid's El Sol team. All the teams he'd played for, wins, athletic accolades, modeling contracts and other endorsements took up most of the page. Being independently wealthy at twenty-nine years old, he had accomplished a lot in his short life. But though everything in his current and future life appeared to be looking rosy, he'd walked away from his career. *Who does that?* That tidbit of mystery was added to the list of why Jesse wouldn't be a suitable substitute for his father.

"This doesn't change my mind. Nothing on this page makes me believe he can finish the job." Irritation tightened Belinda's shoulders, heightening her tension. "This is too much of a big deal and an important part of the rollout to rely on the unknown, even if it's Ed's wish to send his soccer-playing son as a replacement. And did you really read this? Why is he home anyway?" Belinda pushed the paper back to Tawny. "He worked on a few charities. In addition to being a real pro with the soccer ball, he had set a few records with female groupies and celebrities. I'm surprised he had energy to play the game." A man with the sexual stamina of a bull wasn't in her list of requirements. Not even if he had the lean, angular pretty-boy face that could melt away her inhibitions. And what was up with the sensual cast of his lips? Was that a pout, or the natural plump and curve of his mouth? Who knew soccer players were so hot? "This is so not the right man for this job. I need a man with real skills, not a professional panty chaser."

"You are harsh." Tawny laughed hard. Even Belinda's dark, scolding gaze didn't subdue her assistant's amusement. "Based on that photo, he might have just cause to earn that label, though." Tawny pretended to kiss the photo. "Should've seen the pics of him without his shirt. In one magazine spread, he only held a towel in place between his legs. Hello!"

"I didn't pay attention to the picture." *Liar.* "And I don't plan to waste time drooling at a computer screen." *Maybe later.* It still wouldn't change her mind about what she thought of his skills. "He could have one eye in the middle of his forehead, for all I care. I need someone to make *that* happen on time." She pointed at the wall, where various parts of the project still had to be completed. "I need a project manager on-site, someone who can get his team moving and roll up his sleeves, when and if necessary. This is all I care about."

"Ed won't have led you wrong. I'm not the only one who believes in you and what you're doing. You will have a place that is special and a haven for a lot of kids and teenagers. I'm crazy confident that you will."

Belinda heard Tawny's loyalty in her voice. As the project passed each milestone, that enthusiasm and co-ownership of the dream were more than welcomed. She needed to stop calling it a dream. The goal was on the verge of reality. The final stage. She felt through every cell of her body duty-bound to protect her project. As the bad news tumbled out, one item after the other, not even Jesse Santiago's unplanned substitution could put an exclamation point on the sucky morning. By September, Labor Day, the facility would be, should be, opening its full-service programs.

Belinda continued voicing her reservations. "You do realize this write-up of Mr. Sexpot doesn't explain why he's here in upstate New York and why he's now working on his daddy's business."

Tawny shrugged. "He suffered a brutal injury while playing. Now it's too late to do any further digging on the matter. He'll be here soon."

"Okay, Grim Reaper. You said *good news*. It better be darn good."

"Now I'm feeling pressure to appease your grumpiness," Tawny groused, before a wide grin spread across her face.

"Spill. I'm going to need a mimosa instead of this coffee in a hot second." Reluctantly Belinda felt drawn to Tawny's suddenly upbeat attitude.

"Miss Grace is coming over."

"When?" Her smile fumbled and disappeared. Her grandmother didn't *do* visits.

"This morning."

"And you're only telling me now." Belinda fixed her clothes, leveling a glare at Tawny.

Tawny waved away her protests. "She needs to talk to you."

"I don't have time for my grandmother."

"You never do. If you don't call her by nine o'clock…" Tawny looked at her watch. "Yikes. It's nine thirty. Anyway, if you don't call, then you don't get to find out what she wants before she visits."

"Not today. Not in the mood for my grandmother and her commands. And you can stop acting as if you're the president of her fan club."

Tawny remained silent. Wisely.

"Any other news?" Belinda hated to ask.

"I bought a box of donuts."

"That you didn't bring with the coffee." Belinda patted her belly. "Anyway, after that double helping of Chinese food last night, I'm on a diet, at least for the day. Let me get to work since my office will have folks in and out all morning. Only one of them, hopefully my new client, is someone I really want to talk to."

As Tawny left her office and disappeared from view, Belinda yelled, "I'll take one instead of two donuts, please."

"More coffee, too?" Tawny shouted back.

"Yeah. Bring it on." Belinda shifted her mind to pressing matters. She turned on her computer and waited for it to power up. After a series of keystrokes, she pulled up the list of remaining donors. One donor leaving did hurt. Two would cause her to make harsh cuts before the operation manager could start. Contracts with the therapists would be terminated. Training of the horses would be curtailed. And the loss of three donors would cripple her in a matter of months. Who was she kidding? The downfall would happen within weeks. The Dreamweaver Riding Program, her heart and soul, could not be an epic fail. It was the only way she knew how to say sorry.

Chapter 2

"Boss, I just saw Miss Grace park her car." Tawny set down the coffee and donut in front of Belinda and made a quick backtrack to the entrance door.

Belinda slid the plate with the donut off to the side. The cup of coffee could remain. She might need something to keep her hands busy through her grandmother's visit.

She desperately tried to smooth back the loose hair that hung wildly around her face. After her morning ride on her horse in the June humidity, Belinda knew her ponytail holder couldn't maintain control over her hair. Normally, her disheveled appearance didn't bother her. She wasn't one to fuss over wardrobe and makeup. After all, this wasn't an office job. But the next few minutes of her life with her stiff and starched grandmother would cause enough anxiety that she'd wished she dragged out a skirt suit from the deep recess of her closet, dug through the underwear drawer for a pair of panty hose and found a tube of lipstick to quickly sweep over her mouth.

Instead, she groaned after quickly surveying her clothing. It was her standard uniform of black T-shirt and black jeans, kind of a night and day contrast to whatever Grace usually wore. The old lady had to have been off her game at one time in her life. At almost eighty years old and still getting front-page coverage on how fabulous she looked, her grandmother was a fashion icon. Deservedly so, but still.

Belinda wiggled her toes. As a rule, when she came to the office, she stepped out of her boots and left them at the entrance door. The treks back and forth, from the office-barn to the stables, the torn-up dirt around the renovated areas near the riding ring, and general outdoor work pushed the necessity for the rule. Not only did it save the brand-new Berber carpet, it cut down on the strong odors of horse urine, manure, and tack that combined with the hay that would be tracked into the office. Usually, her old pair of sneakers was in the office for her to slip on. Of course, today would be the day that she couldn't find them.

Meanwhile, Tawny, who didn't have many dealings with the stable, could balance herself while walking around the office in her skinny, skyscraper-high heels and flaunting the latest fashion trends. She belonged in New York City, not in the small city of Midway in upstate New York, working in a barn with horses as their closest neighbors.

"Belinda, are you here? It's Grace." Her grandmother's distinctive elocution shot her musings to pieces.

"Good morning, grandma…er…Grace." Belinda rose and headed around the desk, but her grandmother had already marched across the room. That was a good thing. She could keep her shoeless feet a secret for a little while longer.

Her grandmother got everyone in the family to call her "Grace" whenever the subject matter concerned Meadows Media. In the case of Dana, she not only called their grandmother Grace, but also boss. Their special bond had blossomed over several years as Dana worked her way up the ladder, culminating in her leading the company. A strategic move that had been met with resistance by business experts, not to mention a few family members, because of Dana's young age. Belinda's take on the issue remained in full protective support for her cousin, as long as Grace had Dana's full buy-in.

"How are you?" Belinda resumed her seat in the safe zone, behind the desk.

"Good as can be. Still busy even though I'm out in the pastures."

The image of her grandmother whiling away time in a field couldn't have been further from the truth. Grace was still making business deals and her social calendar hadn't shrunk. Grandpa Henry had spilled the latest at the last family dinner.

Belinda probed, "Are you still heading to the office every day? You should enjoy retirement. Take a trip. See the world from beyond corporate offices." She'd consider talking her grandmother into a worldwide trip a major coup. Every chance she got, she pushed the idea.

"Is that what your cousin complains to you about?"

"No." Now Dana was going to kill her for putting Grace on alert. It had taken a while for the former CEO of the family business to step down. Dana had shared how much she looked forward to flexing her leadership muscle without Grace's shadow. Even the staff was coming around to relying on Dana without the constant presence of Grace. The cousins had joked that the complete separation might require Grandpa Henry to kidnap his wife and keep her off the grid for several months.

Grace looked around the office. Then her gaze hovered and settled on the wall behind Belinda. She remained silent. But her gaze shifted over the entire visual presentation of the riding program's trajectory. Though Grace's expression remained stoic, Belinda sensed her grandmother's keen interest.

"Renovations are underway. We still have major work to be done. I'm sure that we'll be ready on opening day." Grace's quiet regard unnerved Belinda.

"Really? That's good news. Who are you using?" Her grandmother slowly slid her glance away from the wall to Belinda. "I did take note that you didn't ask for my help after I sent Santiago to you."

"I used Ed. I felt good with your referral since you've used him on several projects. That was enough of a recommendation."

"He's dependable. Not terribly creative, though, when it came to designing the trellis frames in the garden." She sighed with such regal pretension that

Belinda wanted to snort. "But his work is solid and above par. I wouldn't want anyone else."

Belinda nodded. Now wasn't the time to mention the switch from Ed to Jesse. She had her own misgivings. There was no need to hear her grandmother pile on with her criticisms. No matter what Grace would say, all Belinda would hear was that she wasn't good enough. Out of the three cousins, she was the "rock," per Grace's compliment and with her mother's implicit agreement. Belinda was the solid base to provide support, but lacked Dana's nimble, razor-sharp leadership skills. She'd accepted the evaluation, partially relieved that she didn't have what it took to lead anything, including Meadows Media. As a result, she had remained uninspired to prove her grandmother or mother wrong. Early discussions about starting this business hadn't been met with enthusiastic cheers outside of her cousins, Dana and Fiona.

"Let's go for a walk." Her grandmother stood, smoothing her dress and waiting for her to move.

"Where are we going?" Belinda made a mental promise to kill Tawny if she conveniently had forgotten to tell her about this part of Grace's plan.

"Show me the work that's been done." Grace's attention shifted back to the wall in her office where the full layout and status of the project were mapped out. "I want to see what you've been up to."

Tawny slid into view. Her attempt to nab Grace's focus was as loud as her blue dress with white polka dots.

"Tawny, my dear, hope all is well with you. You're looking quite…modern."

Belinda considered Tawny's mission accomplished.

Her assistant looked beyond giddy over Grace's remark. If she wasn't mistaken, Belinda thought that she saw the young woman dip into a quick curtsy. As expected, Grace, her nose in the air, soaked in the adulation as she passed Tawny.

Bowing down to Grace had never been Belinda's style. That was not to say that her grandmother didn't intimidate the heck out of her. Grace and Grandpa Henry were her substitute parents when hers were too busy pursuing careers and she'd been like a satellite office they'd occasionally visit. That's why, despite Grace's hard-nosed demeanor, Belinda had a soft spot for her grandmother.

Today, however, she'd rather spend the morning tweaking her business plan and schmoozing with potential clients, not escorting Grace on a random tour of the area with the uneasy feeling that there was more to her visit than she'd let on so far. Her grandmother's stern profile provided no hints, even after she stared at Belinda's mismatched socks before she could stuff her feet into the boots.

Belinda led Grace to the golf cart that she drove to get around the property quickly. "Hold on," she said. It was an unnecessary warning, since her grandmother had death grips on her arm and the side of the golf cart. She drove slowly down the road that led from the barn to the larger area dedicated to the riding rings and stable.

"Have you ever considered selling off some of the property?"

"No!" Belinda uttered a shaky, apologetic laugh and repeated the negative in a softened tone.

"It's not an outrageous question."

They'd stopped at the stable. Belinda rounded the cart to assist Grace.

"I'm asking because you have ambitions that don't match your pocket." Grace stopped short at the large wooden doors that led into the stables. Her nose twitched as the signature ammonia smell of horse and hay hit them.

Through these doors was magic, the place that brought Belinda peace and joy. She headed over to the stall that was home to her American quarter horse. From the start, Lucky Ducky, her own personal mount, had held a special place in her heart. When she was first looking for horses for the program, her network of business owners with similar equine-therapy services advised her that the retired show horse was up for sale. While she'd need therapy horses for now, she wanted her own horse. It was this gelding's gentle nature and agility that convinced her that she was on the right path with her decision to acquire a member of this breed.

Grace joined her at Lucky Ducky's stall. "Are you a bit over your head with this monster-size project?"

"I can manage. I've been managing." Belinda hoped that she'd retained a knack for reading her grandmother's trains of thought. Although, sometimes, she wasn't sure that she ever had the ability and only had mastered feeling defensive.

From her pocket, Grace withdrew sugar cubes, which she fed to the grateful horse. Despite her grandmother's reaction to the stable, she was a wet noodle around the chestnut gelding. Belinda wished she could take a secret photo of her grandmother making kissing noises. Lucky Ducky certainly loved Grace's attention. His head bumped against her hand to make her continue scratching his muzzle.

"Why are we here…in the barn?" Belinda walked over to a new horse that she'd bought two weeks ago. She'd rather have waited on buying another horse, but, by acquiring him, she had rescued a pet that the owner could no longer afford to keep. She grabbed a brush and stroked Black Pearl's powerful side with it. His head bobbed as he pranced in place.

"We needed to talk. And since you don't have a proper office…" Grace pointedly looked over at her. "We must stand out here for privacy."

No matter how much Grace worked Belinda's nerves, being disrespectful was never an option. "No, we don't have to, Grandma. Let's go up to the house. I have tea."

"Okay, for the house. No, on the tea."

"It's not the regular supermarket tea." Belinda offered Grace a hint of a smile. "Herbal. Rooibos from South Africa."

Grace clapped her hands. "What are you waiting for? Let's go." She bid farewell to Lucky Ducky with an extra sugar cube and accompanied Belinda out of the stable.

Her grandmother resumed her death grip as they rode the golf cart eastward across the property.

On a small hill, the farmhouse stood out, its exterior painted in sunshine yellow accented with winter-white shutters. The morning sunrise was an amazing sight that climbed above the mountains in the distance.

Belinda gazed on her little home with pride. Well, it wasn't so little, with five bedrooms ranging from a closet-size one to the master suite. Though many of the rooms were unused, here was the house for her future. One day, she wanted it full of children and a loving husband.

Given her lack of a social life, however, said loving husband would have to magically fall from the sky in front of her like an airdrop package.

"Have a seat. I'll bring it to you." Belinda motioned toward the living area before walking into the kitchen.

"No need to wait on me. I'll follow you to your kitchen."

Belinda hoped that the kitchen wasn't a mess. The bad part about living alone was that any messiness could only be blamed on her. She cringed as she watched her grandmother swing her survey around the room before she took a seat at the four-seater table.

"You haven't been to visit, much less sit in my kitchen, in a while. I'm nervous." Belinda couldn't deal with waiting for Grace to reveal the reason for her impromptu visit. There was no way that this was a casual visit.

"I've been remiss with keeping up with my grandchildren. Turning over Meadows Media to Dana was a bigger deal than I thought. It made me think about all of you. Our legacy as a family."

"Dana's doing fine, right?"

"Oh, yes. Dana was born for that job."

"Proud of her." Belinda always knew that her cousin was the only one to step into Grace's shoes. Her mother and aunts, Grace's daughters, grumbled a bit, but no one could deny that Dana had the brains and passion to take up the heavy responsibility.

"We all are. Meadows Media should always remain in the family."

Belinda carefully set down the steaming cup of tea. "I'm not coming to work for Meadows Media." For once, she wasn't backing down. Not even to look away from Grace's deep-set eyes.

"Not even for Dana?"

"Did she ask for me?" Belinda wasn't biting, though the mention of her cousin needing her gave her pause.

"You know your cousin. She'd never ask for help. She's too afraid that it would reflect on her. However, since stepping back from it all, I have a good view from the sidelines. What I see, in my overall vision, is for all of you cousins stepping up and taking your rightful places in the company. Making it bigger and better. Besides, you get along with each other. That's half the battle."

"What if the cousins aren't interested?"

"Why wouldn't you be? I built this company to hand down, not to sell out. Not that my three daughters ever stepped up to the plate." Grace sniffed. The woman was a born queen and didn't need a title to go with her mostly formidable demeanor. The one subject that could tighten that mouth and send the lines in her forehead into deeper grooves was her daughters—their mothers.

Away from the Meadows family home estate, away from the Meadows Media headquarters, Belinda had never heard Grace open up with such a sad, longing commentary. Took a visit, while sitting at her dining table, for the intimate disclosure. Anytime Grace's tale was told in front of an audience, the rags to riches story had all the polish and shiny glint of a spin doctor's touch. Not that her accomplishments were make-believe. However, Grace believed that imperfections of any sort belonged behind the family wall of privacy and loyalty. It was the one trait that was supported by every family member as a united front.

"Look, Belinda, the time is right. Dana is on the verge of taking the company to new heights. Kent is on board. Hopefully, they'll be married soon. You're turning thirty-one this year. I couldn't be happier with all that you've done."

"I'm running *my* own business here."

"I'm not taking away from your plans. Not one bit." Grace leaned in and took her hand. "I'm expanding on what you have."

Belinda tried to avoid her hypnotic stare. Instead, she looked down at her hand still captured by Grace. Her grandmother's rings and bracelets shimmered as the light caught the diamonds and bounced off the gold. The older woman wasn't exactly touchy-feely. So to have her hands imprisoned in her grandmother's firm grasp made her want to clutch on to something else and hang on for dear life.

"Come work for Meadows. I'll give you the money to fix this place into what you want and hire a full staff. You don't have to be here."

Money, the one thing that she desperately needed, landing in her lap. Hers for the taking. If only her stomach didn't constrict at the idea. Her heart instantly ached at the steep price to her dream. Although the proposal came with a win-win solution—money and the riding program—she didn't like it because of the sacrifice to her independence.

"I see you're ready to say no." Grace patted her hand. "Don't jump into the deep end to show that you can."

"I have something here. It's important to me. At a young age, you had something that was important. We've all benefited from it. But Meadows Media isn't for me." Belinda stood and hoped that her legs would stop shaking. "And there is nothing more to discuss, Grandma." This wasn't business. It was personal. "I've got to return to the office. I'm expecting someone."

Even the unsuitable Jesse Santiago would be a welcomed diversion.

"You've got moxie, kid." Grace chuckled. She braced herself with her walking stick and pushed up from the chair. "I'll mark my calendar. Same time, same place, next month—I'll make the offer again. By then, reality might have a way of nipping at your heels." The gravelly voice laid down the somber forecast.

Belinda nodded. A faint whiff of victory danced a fleeting pattern with her ego because Grace's prediction had that edge of inevitability. But she'd take the victory lap and enjoy it. "I'll drive you to your car."

Grace nodded. Signs of sentimentality vanished with her stiff march to the front door. She pulled it open before Belinda could reach for the doorknob.

"Oh, hello. Who might you be?" Her grandmother effectively blocked Belinda's view.

"Jesse Santiago, ma'am." The man's deep, crisp voice hooked Belinda's attention.

"Grace Meadows, here." Handshakes were exchanged.

Belinda tried to see around her grandmother's formidable stature.

"Santiago? You must be Ed's son." Grace turned her head slightly toward Belinda and finished, "Devilishly handsome, this one."

Good grief, her grandmother's abrupt switch to playfulness embarrassed her. However, if she felt the need to comment, then maybe the subject on hand was worth a look-see. Belinda couldn't deal with any trigger to tap her emotions out of sleep mode and distract her from the Dreamweaver facility. This man had better have the skill set to impress the heck out of her.

In the meantime, she really wished Grace would move out of the doorway.

"Now, be sure to say hello to your father. I've sent a fruit basket to the house."

"Thank you. I'm sure he'll be pleased."

So Grace knew about Ed's health issues and his son taking on the job. Now she wondered if that was why Grace seized on the timing to put in an appearance to pressure her to work at Meadows Media. It was too much to figure out, right now. Time for the big reveal at her front door. All she could see were his faded jeans and scuffed construction boots.

"Make sure you do a good job for my granddaughter, young man."

"Yes, ma'am."

Belinda heaved a sigh of relief when Grace finally walked out through the doorway. Under the direct light of the morning sun, Jesse Santiago moved center stage into the frame. Wow. Now, that was tall, as, with her five-nine height, she still had to look up. Thick black hair framed the top of his head in a trimmed style that enhanced the attractive contours of his squared jaw and high cheekbones.

His hands were pushed down in the front pockets. Head tilted to the side. While his eyes remained hidden behind dark shades, her attention was transferred to the slender, prominent line of his nose. Her continued admiration landed on his mouth, the one feature that she'd lingered on in the photo, and it looked better in real life. Now she could verify that he had wide, full lips that were pure sexy. His pose didn't shift under her perusal. In fact, he looked casual, but in control.

"Your assistant sent me over here."

Belinda stepped out of her house and closed the door. "I've got to take my grandmother to her car. Mind meeting me back at the office? We can chat there." She shook his hand and continued on her path to the golf cart where Grace waited.

He was handsome as all get-out, had a firm handshake and smelled like heaven. Having this man around would be tempting. If she didn't stay on point, she'd do silly things like give him a second or third look. Because, that fast, she already connected to whatever wildly charged energy he exuded.

Crazy. It was not happening, even if the electricity shot in one direction, from her to him.

"Child, no need to kill me on the way to my car."

"Sorry." Belinda didn't realize that she pressed on the accelerator, jostling her grandmother in the process.

"Trust me. He's not going anywhere. He'll be there after you drop me off. I don't think he took his eyes off you once."

Belinda deliberately brushed off the remark. The strange ping of excitement blipped on her romantic radar. "Good seeing you, Grandma."

"Hmm. As I said, I'll be back."

Belinda waited until her grandmother drove away before she made a U-turn back to the office and pushed down on the accelerator. One thought muscled past her body's silly reactions to this stranger. How would she stay focused, with Jesse Santiago sabotaging her steely determination with such übersexy maleness?

Chapter 3

Belinda stood outside the office for a few seconds to get herself together. Being outed by her grandmother was a bit like someone pointing out a pimple on her forehead, an embarrassing fact that didn't need to be put on blast. The best solution would be to ignore him as much as she could after she acknowledged that Jesse looked good from head to toe. She would file her reaction under Do-Not-Entertain Thoughts and move on to the matter on hand—the equine-therapy center.

She kicked off her boots and padded in her socks past Tawny. Her assistant held up several full-size printed pages of Jesse, some solo, some with a female companion. She gave a thumbs-up gesture, which Belinda ignored. Despite being in full agreement that, yes, the man was more than just handsome, fine, drop-dead gorgeous, she refused to confirm it. With the last photo of him on her mind, Belinda stepped into her office.

"Oh…" She couldn't help feeling flustered. With all those thumbs-up signs, Tawny didn't bother to give any indicators that he was already here.

Belinda stepped farther into the office and took notice of the small details about him. He sat back in the chair which was turned slightly outward as if he waited for her to enter. While some salespersons came on business in a nervous and eager state, this man owned his calm demeanor. Meanwhile, he cupped the bottle of antacids from her desk in his hands, before repeatedly tossing it in the air. His gaze never left her face, except for a casual once-over when she walked toward him.

In the small space, the disturbing wild energy she'd sensed from him before grew more intense. Close up, the man was more than handsome with his rich, brown skin, striking features and tall stature. His voice hadn't been hard on the ears, either. Cool and casual seemed to be his signature style, as if the only place that he'd break a sweat was on the soccer field. The dark shades he wore and kept on in her office tossed in a bit of mystery, an attitude that somehow he was detached from, and bored by, the world of regular folk.

"Is the light bothering you?" she pointedly asked. It was time to get down to business. Not being able to read him wasn't his fault, but that didn't make it better.

He shook his head and removed the glasses. He blinked. Or maybe she did, several times. The corner of his mouth hitched into a half smile. He tossed out the net, and she got caught. *Gotcha.*

Gray eyes with hints of olive and amber. Thick, dark lashes to go with the heavy eyebrows. *Put the glasses back on.* Now her admiration volleyed between the deep-set eyes and his mouth. In between the points of her indecision, the angles and planes of his cheek and chin were chiseled to perfection. Once more, he blinked and her stomach did a flip. She had to cut that out. Right now, her mind was a little preoccupied and her body reacted accordingly like a starved woman at a buffet.

No wonder he had females ready to lose their common sense. Falling under his spell sounded far-fetched in the gossip magazines. But when the subject sat in the chair a few feet away looking like God's gift, the reality certainly had a different spin. Her recommendation—he needed a warning label.

She wouldn't react to him only if she was dead or celibate, and since neither applied, she stood the chance of succumbing to Jesse Santiago fever. Those good looks had to be all window dressing. She remained unconvinced that there was anything of substance behind the rock-hard physique.

He broke the silence. "Didn't realize that I was working with Grace Meadows."

"You're not," Belinda responded with deliberate sharpness. "You're working for me." And that new arrangement wasn't a given, although it had moved from "heck no" to serious consideration.

"That's what I thought until I met Mrs. Meadows. Cool lady." His mouth twitched. Not really a smile.

Again with the casual tilt of the head—he was studying her.

"She is." Belinda settled into her seat. "Would you like coffee?" she offered. Personally, between the coffee and tea, she would float away with another cup.

"No. I'm good."

She nodded. No argument there. Time to get down to business. Sharing her vision would be the best way to figure out if Jesse had what it took to do the job. She'd listen to him weigh in on the plans, then she'd evaluate his potential contribution.

Although construction was near the midpoint of completion, Belinda started her presentation with what had been accomplished and her expectation of the final facility. Several times, she paused to see if he was onboard. He said nothing, but sat poised, leaning forward. Maybe he was a silent thinker.

"That's it in a nutshell." She closed her speech by turning his attention to the final mock-up of her facility in full use with trainers, horses and children.

"A lot of kids are in need of such a place?"

"Yes. Unfortunately, there is a need. And more doctors and therapists are agreeing on the effectiveness of this alternative."

Again, the silent regard. Unnerving.

Belinda reiterated, "The project must be completed by September."

"Really?" He pushed himself out of the chair and strode around the desk.

Remaining in her chair set her at a disadvantage. It didn't help that his hips were too close to her eye level. The jeans, even with the way they loosely draped his lower body, couldn't diminish certain assets. Re-

tirement had not reduced him to a squishy mound
of flesh. The corded muscles of his forearms, with
tattoos winding around one limb, provided a visual
sampler of a man who once seemed fond of celebrating his goals with a massive roar while gripping his
soccer shirt in one hand.

Thanks, Tawny, for flashing me that photo treat.

"Barely three months to finish." Now he looked
closely at her vision board.

"Is that a problem?" She stood and matched his
crossed-arms stance.

"Why are you building such a large riding ring?
Plus, you're adding a building."

"Renovating," she corrected, not liking his accu-
satory tone.

"A lot of horses."

"A lot of children."

He frowned. "Thought it was also a horse-training
stable for jumping."

"Why would you think so?"

"I figured you competed. You've got the body for
it." He spread his arms wide and offered the first real
smile she'd seen with a flash of bright white. "Just
being on the up-and-up. No harm. No foul."

Immediately, her cheeks warmed. The compliment
rushed at her like a rogue wave and covered her in
tingly excitement. But enough willpower kicked in to
keep her from giggling like a nitwit.

"You'd wear those skintight pants. The little black
helmet tied under your chin." He grinned. "I've seen
it on TV."

"Are you quite finished?"

He opened his mouth to respond.

She waved off any further trek down this strange, winding path. "Don't answer that."

"Hey, I'm just paying you a compliment." He returned to his seat and settled in, resting his elbows on his knees. "I see the brains with all of that on the wall and the beauty right in front of me."

"Thanks." Holding off this man and his penchant for flirtation needed to be handled like ripping off a Band-Aid. "Cheesy compliments are unnecessary."

"But, I'm sure they were not unwelcome." Again, the smile flashed.

Did he wink his left eye? Her gaze narrowed. Unfortunately, her body's reaction wanted to listen to his drivel. Her cheeks hadn't cooled down over his last comments, and the temperature in the room had escalated a notch.

Belinda struggled to stay on firm ground. "You do realize this is an interview."

He shrugged.

"Don't know? Or don't care?"

"I'm open to whatever you may need."

"What I need is someone who is serious about working. What I want is for this job to be completed on time." Talking about her dream project was the perfect wall to ward off the effects of his flirtation. "Are you up for the job?"

"My father seems to think so."

"You sound doubtful."

"Not really. I'm holding down the job until Dad gets better."

Belinda didn't care for his plain speak, in this instance. "Because you may head back to playing soccer?"

Light to dark. Amusement to irritation. Expressions flitted across his face, accompanied by the stiff set of his shoulders. A nerve had been plucked. It was accidental on her part, though, since she didn't know enough about him to judge potential landmines.

"My only plan right now is to help out with projects," he replied with a measured tone. "Yours included."

In other words, she had to back away from soccer chitchat.

"Do you mind if I get a cup of water?" He headed for the nearby cooler before she nodded. "You?"

"Sure. Thank you. I should've offered." Belinda waited for Jesse to bring the water. This man intrigued her, with his steady level of confidence evident as he moved around her office. Despite him being off the field, his body appeared fit. Even her inexperienced eye spotted the overall well-toned physique. Her imagination guessed that the rest of him was equally hard and ripped. She couldn't stop recalling the photo of Jesse celebrating a goal with his shirt off. Sweaty and victorious looked damned good on him.

"Here ya go." He handed her the cup.

She carefully took the drink from him, afraid to touch his hand, no matter how briefly. There was no need for a repeat of the shock to her system that had taken her by surprise. She sipped the water in an attempt to cool her emotional jets. "Let's get back to our discussion. This is a personal endeavor that has nothing to do with equestrian competition or training show horses. Far from it. It's about bringing joy and changing the lives of a special group of children through the use of horses." She wanted him to understand. Otherwise, there could be no business connection between them.

"Is there a great need for this type of business? In this area?" His continued doubt poured out with each question.

"Whether I help one person or twenty, it's worth it. Do you have any experience with working on stables, riding rings, fences?"

"Yeah."

She waited for further explanation. None seemed to be forthcoming. "How did you learn?"

"My father. Shoulder to shoulder, we worked on a lot of things when I was younger. I can show you all my scars." He raised his hands and flicked them to show the back, and then the palms, of his hands. No scars or calluses were visible. Instead, she noted the long, blunt fingers with veins and muscles leading up to lean forearms. "These hands have seen a lot of action." He interlocked said hands and rested them on his lap.

A lot of action. Her truth? She loved a man's hands. You could see strength and beauty, gentleness and caring—all necessary parts of a man's character—there. Her analysis had never steered her wrong. Nice hands meant a sensitive touch, from casual communication to intimate cuddling, sexy foreplay and beyond.

Belinda took another sip of water.

"What have been some recent projects that you've worked on?"

"I've helped out my father on several assignments around town. There was nothing that I couldn't do." His blasé tone turned curt, precise. "And references aren't a problem." His cell phone rang with a horrendous series of chimes. He looked at the screen and pushed to connect. "Do you mind if I get this?"

Belinda waved him on.

With the phone at his ear, he strolled out the office.

After Jesse left to take his call, Belinda worried. In all the scenarios of her dreams, she'd never envisioned the project incomplete. The image of things unraveling made her panicky. And the arrival on the scene of Jesse, equipped with more blatant sex appeal than possible construction management expertise, didn't quiet her unease.

Waiting for him to finish his call, all she could do was take a seat, cross her arms and stare at the timeline. One option would be to wait for Ed to recuperate and get the facility built to her specifications without drama. Another option was finding another contractor, but Dreamweaver Riding Program had a scheduled start date in three months. And nothing so far was supporting that time frame. She reached for the bottle of antacids.

"And where the hell is Tawny?" Belinda muttered. Her assistant had the knack of calming her. As she exited her office to look for Tawny, she heard Jesse still on the phone. By now, she didn't care if he had a call. He was on her time. But there wasn't any sign of him.

Instead of holding his call in the office, apparently he'd taken the call outside. Before she took another step, his voice escalated. It was intense, possibly angry. She froze.

"I'm not going to change my mind. Olivier, it's been over. Chapter closed. A documentary on my life? Are you kidding me?" Jesse's laugh held little humor. "Not happening because I know it's going to somehow get twisted in my supposed comeback as the final point of this publicity stunt to get the fans worked up. I don't need the pressure." His footsteps marked the small area.

Belinda pressed against the wall. Her heart thudded its rapid drumbeat.

Not until she heard his feet resume their pacing did she exhale. His angry statements were now indecipherable mumbles. She inched closer, pushing away any guilt at eavesdropping. She would save feeling guilty for when she was caught. To hear him so agitated shocked her. What happened to his casual cockiness?

"Pop is on the mend. At home, grumbling. Driving Mom crazy." There was a mix of a snort and chuckle. "I'm safer on the outside of Santiago and Sons Construction. That's Diego's domain. I pop in when needed." He paused for a while. "Call me all the names you want. I'm not meeting with anyone to be browbeaten. I get enough of that here." He quieted, even his pacing slowing until he stood still. "For your information, I'm on a job. With horses. Yes, horses— smell and all! Stop laughing. I can smell the stable a mile away."

Belinda was interested, now that the heated conversation had turned to her business.

"The owner? She's cool. A bit over the top with all these plans." His pacing brought him closer to her hiding spot. "What do I think?"

Silence.

"Of her? Man, I'm not heading down that road. Stop laughing. Okay, she's not hard on the eyes. Bumpin' body. Got a smile that can light up a dark room. See…right there, you've got me talking non-sense. I'm going to be busy with my demons. Not on board for anything. End of that discussion."

"What are you doing?"

Belinda almost jumped out of her skin when Tawny whispered in her ear. "Shh."

Now they both listened.

"I know that she wants my father, not me, on the job. Too bad Diego is working on a project for the mayor's office." He paused. "In the meantime, I'll push around the hay until Pop's back. Then I'll move on to find my next chapter."

His feet shuffled closer. Belinda backed up, pushing Tawny away from the area.

"Thanks for the heads-up about the documentary. I'm sure my agent will be lighting up my phone. Bye."

Belinda continued pushing Tawny ahead of her as they hurried back to her desk. They made it to her office before Jesse rounded the corner. Tawny froze into position with an exaggerated lean over the paper-work on the desk. Meanwhile, Belinda pointed to a random spot on the paper. By the time Jesse entered, Tawny came to life and nodded, as if in agreement with a point they'd discussed.

"Done with my call. Sorry about that." He didn't walk over to the desk. Instead, he remained in the doorway. The way his face was set meant that he hadn't shaken off the effects of his call.

Belinda stepped away from Tawny. Regardless of the chiseled good looks, she only had one message for him. "Mr. Santiago—"

"Jesse."

She ignored the casual interjection. "Upon careful consideration, I will only work with your father. The bid was accepted based on his ability to do the job. *His* reputation is pretty stellar. I respect how he treated the project, and how he managed the team to stay on task. I knew what I was getting and wasn't ever disappointed." Deliberately pausing to deliver the closing blow, she clasped her hands. In a soft, but frigid tone, she finished, "In other words, Jesse, I'm not interested in using you as a substitute. I will be making alternative arrangements for another company to take over. Of course, this will delay my plans. Quite unexpected, although I realize that it was unforeseen. This program is important and I want the best. Having you *push around hay* is the last thing that I'm going to settle for."

"What?"

"Have a good day. I've got to get back to some pressing matters." Belinda returned to sit behind her desk.

Tawny had turned into a statue. Her gaze locked on to Belinda. Her eyes open wide, her expression frozen.

"When is the next appointment, Tawny?"

"Um…now," her assistant squeaked. "I'll go… maybe they're here…now." Tawny sidled her way out of Belinda's office, probably to the safe zone of her own area. Belinda was too irritated over the situation to find the humor in Tawny's comedic contortions to avoid looking at Jesse.

At first, Belinda thought she'd have to be the first to make a move. He hadn't budged. Plan B was to get up and leave him in her office until he got the message that she meant business. Although stomping out in socks didn't have the same kiss-my-behind vibe that she'd want.

Finally, he shifted out of his stance. Without making a big deal or pretending to give a damn, he shrugged and left. She stared at the empty space he left behind. The tumultuous energy of anger and sexual attraction evaporated, sucked out with his departure. In its wake, something akin to disappointment settled softly into place. For the first time since she started this company, she'd fired someone. Well, she hadn't hired him. A mere technicality.

"Thanks for nothing, Jesse Santiago."

Chapter 4

Fired.

Jesse had never been fired in his life. Not even during his days as a paperboy tossing the weekend newspapers onto many rooftops and into trees. Not during his college days when he slept through the night shift as campus security. Yet in less than an hour, the woman whom he had every intention to pursue, despite his misgivings, had not only overheard his uncensored tirade, but had also kicked his behind to the curb. The fact that she didn't waste time working things out, negotiating, or compromising with him stung like a slap to the face.

People in his professional sports life always contorted to please him. He was used to hearing "no problem" to any of his requests. His superstar skills on the soccer field elevated his status. From athlete to model, his personal stock soared—the money flowed and his circle of friends widened to include celebrities, rock stars and even politicians. During those days, the ladies always came and went. Some stuck around longer than others, depending on if they thought he'd end his bachelorhood for them. Being treated as a thing, rather than a person, had become the norm. Sometimes, he, in turn, made the same mistake. From the beginning, he'd underestimated Belinda Toussaint.

This lady shone with a special light of natural beauty. Though she wore no discernible makeup, Belinda looked flawless. Normally, beauty alone characterized the women who followed him after the games. Belinda was different. Her face openly communicated her feelings, a trait he found refreshing. He didn't peg her as the type to swoon for him with raunchy comments and come-hither winks. Although she was statuesque and curvaceous in all the right places, he was more attracted to her intelligence and determination. Fire raged in her dark brown eyes, deep-set and piercing, as she talked about her project. That intensity came at him like a loud call to something exciting.

It jarred him. A lot. And he wanted to feel that new buzz again. Somehow, he had to make amends with Belinda to continue his exploration through the unknown.

Since his days in elite soccer, nothing came close to holding his attention. The business and its mission sounded like a huge undertaking, but not keeping a lockdown on his thoughts gave the wrong impression. He did care. His habit of shrugging off commitments, personal and business, landed him in a sticky mess.

"Damn it! I got fired." Jesse pulled into his parents' driveway.

His gut tightened as he pushed the car gear into Park. He tried his best to come up with a story to tell his father that wasn't a lie, but danced around the recent epic fail. Maybe he simply could break the news separately to each parent. Better for his eardrums. His father would take it all in without asking too many questions or revealing the direction of his thoughts. Jesse often joked that he was like Confucius. But when his father did deliver his opinion, Jesse wouldn't have a doubt Ed was angry.

His mother, on the other hand, would escalate the offense with the lungs of a vendor at an open-air market. She would be shouting, or according to her— speaking for the hardheaded—and lecturing until he begged her to stop.

As for Diego, his brother would rip through him. It would be nice to have a default brother to commit bigger offenses. The job of screwup belonged to him. Jesse expected that his brother's hot temper would be in full force. One day, they'd hash out the troubles that had long been brewing between them. What he didn't want was for this particular development to ignite a bigger brouhaha between them. Then Diego would push to take over the project with Belinda. That was not happening, if he could help it.

Time to set things straight. He opened the car door and stepped out. The front door swung open and his father waved him in with a bright smile.

"Hey, son. Didn't think I'd see you until later. Must be my lucky day because I just got off the phone with Diego." His father hugged him. Although the old man had heart problems and was supposed to be in bed,

Ed was clearly up and about in the house. Of course, Jesse's mother wasn't home to scold him.

"Dad, you should be resting."

"Ah...never mind about me. I saw you sitting in the driveway. Figured that I'd surprise you with how well I'm doing." As Jesse saw him up close, fatigue had sucked some of the vitality from his body. A dusky pallor tinted his father's skin. "Your brother is working hard around the clock. Too much, if you ask me, 'cause your mother and I haven't seen him in a while." His father patted his arm. "Well, you're here. Like old times."

Not quite like old times, because he didn't visit home often.

"I figured I'd stop in." Jesse followed him into the family room.

His father settled in with a few groans and a dismissive slap at his assistance. Jesse opted for the sofa next to him and stretched out his legs, pretending to be relaxed, a demeanor that he'd perfected.

Ed looked over the rim of his glasses. "I know that I came down hard on you last night. It was one of those father-son talks that sounded more like a lecture than advice."

"It's okay, Pop."

"You're an adult, free to make up your mind about your career. Shouldn't have lost my head. You'll make the correct decision when the time is right." Ed scratched his head. Despite not having to deal with baldness, his father opted to shave his hair. He figured it was the best way to take care of the gray. Either way, his father was a handsome man with a touch of resemblance to Quincy Jones, a heavily biased assessment that he freely acknowledged.

"I didn't come home to make you worry. I just needed a break. And then I'll find something to anchor me."

"I don't want you to feel depressed. This is a blip on the timeline. You know what I mean." His father smiled and Jesse responded with a grin. What else could he do?

His father continued, "You're back, but you're not really. Your mom thinks you're moping around over a woman. She thinks that someone broke your heart." Ed pushed up his glasses.

"No girlfriends. No drama." Jesse really did try to avoid the trap of having his personal life on display in the tabloids. It would only take one hanger-on's teary-eyed accusation claiming he'd promised they would be together to make him whip out a no-strings-attached relationship contract. Although he was home, away from the limelight, he still didn't want to mess with its unpredictable landscape.

"Okay. Your mother may have something to say about that." His father pointed at his own chest. "I, on the other hand, think there is more than a woman weighing on your mind. My guess is that soccer is still in your heart."

Jesse shook his head.

"It's in your blood."

Jesse remained silent. That was the same argument the team used to lure him back. In his defense, he'd say their expectation needed an adjustment. He was an ordinary man.

He reached over and picked up a framed photo of

the family—his parents and Diego smiling for the studio portrait with its standard blue-gray backdrop. Simpler times. Happier. The last official family portrait that included him was from about five years ago. The oversize portrait hung on the wall in the living room. In the remainder of the house, signs of his absence were plentiful. It hurt. Pinpricks to the heart. He set down the frame on the side table.

"When you're ready to talk, I'm here." Ed sighed, long and deep. "Where else am I going? My heart is like a temperamental clock that can't keep the time. It makes me grumpy. So give me some good news. Tell me about this morning's appointment with Belinda." Ed's grin showered him with fatherly pride and confidence.

Jesse's guilt pulled up a chair to sit for the solo act. "Pop, I've got to tell you something."

"Yeah?"

"The job…at Belinda's. Miss Toussaint." Jesse cleared his throat. Oh man, this was tough. Maybe he should have reached for his father's scotch and poured a double shot.

"Spit it out. Did you see her plans? That young lady is all kinds of awesome." Again, the proud grin appeared, the corners of his eyes crinkled with delight.

"Oh, there he goes again." His mother came through the back door by way of the garage. Her arms were laden with grocery bags. "Your father is an admirer of Grace's granddaughters, every last one of them. But I think he's got a soft spot especially for Belinda," she joked. Her loud chuckle accompanied her retreat to the pantry.

Jesse hurried to assist his mom. He planted a kiss

on her cheek poised for his attention. "You bought my favorite." He spied the package of chocolate chip cookies. After the morning he had, cookies and chocolate milk sounded ideal. But he still hadn't forgotten the reason for the shot of scotch.

"Belinda is a respectful lady," Ed continued to press his point with his booming voice that reached them in the kitchen.

Jesse remained silent, pretending to be intently occupied with stocking the pantry shelves. He didn't question any of his father's praise for his client. The more Jesse heard, the more his guilt multiplied. He rubbed his forehead. Now he'd have to admit his mistake with his mother present. Knowing his father was the president of Belinda's fan club might earn him a thump in the head. Sympathy for his old soccer injuries wouldn't get him out of this. His mother, however, might throw the large can of baked beans for a one-shot knockout.

His father slowly walked in, much slower now that his mother was home. He leaned heavily against the counter. "Jesse will work on Belinda's project. He went there this morning to iron out the details." His father's voice swelled with pride. "Grace won't be the only one with a family business."

"Really? You're going to handle the job?" Caroline beamed. No doubt her circle of friends would learn the news on Facebook before the day's end. "My sons are so hardworking like their pop. I'm glad you're home, Jesse." She reached over and gently cupped his cheek. "I've missed you."

Jesse nodded—well, not actually. His chin bobbed and then he stretched his neck, offering no commitment. Now that he was home, there was an adjustment period to rejoin and blend into the family routine.

Instead, in a short time, he'd caused a crisis. At the mention of Grace's name, he realized a bit late that angering her wasn't smart, even if unintentional. Not only had he lost this contract, but his faux pas could affect Ed's relationship with Grace. He hadn't thought that far ahead. All he had thought about was how much he hated not being in control, losing his cool and being a jerk in Belinda's office.

Jesse offered, "I have a few more meetings with Belinda and then we'll get started." Hopefully, it would buy him time to go hat in hand to Belinda and ask for his job back.

"Good. You know I'm here if you need me. My brain is still working." His father sat on the kitchen barstool.

"Jesse, please remind your father that he may not get a second chance if he doesn't follow the doctor's orders." His mom scrunched her nose. "He's not the best patient."

"Doctor says, I'll be up and about in another week. I can join you then."

"Depending on the test results," his mother piped up.

Jesse nodded. "Looking forward to it."

"Well, while my favorite guys are talking shop, I'm going to get these steaks on the grill."

Jesse's stomach rumbled appreciatively. Breathing a bit easier, he settled down next to his father to watch an old classic movie back in the family room. By tomorrow, everything would be fixed, and no one would know what a mess he'd made.

* * *

Later that night after he had hung out at his parents', Jesse headed home. His mother pressed him to stay at the house, arguing that the place was empty and needed younger blood to give it energy. Staying with them wasn't a matter of how it would look, but more about him needing his space. At the end of the day, he enjoyed unwinding on the houseboat. Well, most days it was fun. Sometimes, the nights did get to him, since being alone with only his thoughts for company wasn't always relaxing. Not when doubts and second-guessing crowded his mind that he'd made the wrong decision about his career.

Instead of heading to the marina, Jesse changed his route and headed across the city limits. It was time to get things out in the open between him and Diego. It might be a blindside, but he didn't want to drag out the inevitable discussion. Maybe dropping in without warning would prevent his brother from brushing him off.

He pulled up at Diego's town house. Good. The lights were on. If his brother was entertaining, then things might get awkward. He'd retreat and come at this another day. Taking a deep breath, he walked up and pushed the doorbell. Almost immediately, Diego opened the door.

"Hey, what's up?"

"On my way home. Thought I'd stop by." Jesse shrugged. "Talk…"

Diego stepped back.

Jesse entered and headed toward the living room. "Hope I'm not interrupting."

"You're not." Diego had closed the front door, but didn't move.

"Got a beer?"

"I don't drink. Iced tea?"

"Sure." Jesse sat and rubbed his hands on his thighs. Tension rolled in, affecting the mood.

Diego returned with the beverage. "It's late."

"Pop was asking for you today." Jesse tried for a safe subject.

"The mayor's project is running into snags. I'm there from early morning until late. Got in not too long ago."

Jesse nodded. Now that he really looked at his brother, Diego did look wilted around the edges. The pristine, Ivy League image had been replaced with someone who looked, well, normal. His hair was unkempt. Signs of more than a five o'clock shadow covered the lower half of his face. Even his build had a little bump-out with muscles.

People said they almost looked like twins, except for the four-year age difference. They were close. Or used to be. Diego outdid himself academically, while soccer took over Jesse's life from high school onward. They lived with no regrets. At least, that was the family mantra that motivated him on his journey.

"I won't stay long." Jesse hadn't touched the drink. It was to buy him time to figure out the best approach.

"What do you want, Jesse?"

"That's direct."

"Yeah, well…"

"What's with the attitude? I had better conversations with you when I was in Spain. Since I've been back, you're treating me like the enemy. If I said something to offend you, let me know. But I'm walking on egg shells. I don't get it." Jesse felt like he'd sprinted to the finish line. "Would you at least take a seat? I feel like you're about to throw me out."

Diego remained standing. "You always want things your way. You left and I stayed. We both pursued our dreams. But I didn't forget where I came from. I didn't replace my family."

"Replace? What on earth are you saying?"

"I watched you grow more distant with the family. The more success you had, the less we saw you. Your inner circle became your family. Mom and Dad praised you, made excuses when you changed your plans to come home for the holidays. Then you hit Spain as the young phenom, and we barely heard from you. I had to look at the sports channel to get the updates."

"You've got it all wrong." Jesse cringed at his brother's condemnation.

"Why? Because you always get it right. You left without looking back. That, I learned to deal with. But don't expect that since you tumbled off the throne, you can rewrite history and act like you weren't a jerk, that you didn't want to belong to Midway. The family."

"Stop right there. I may be a lot of things, but I have never been ashamed of my family. You don't have a clue what I went through."

"You're right, I don't. And that's something you made sure of."

"Look, I came here to talk. Instead, you're on me like an attack dog." Jesse stood. "I'm not sure why your view is so skewed. I called. I came when I could. I paid off the mortgage, so Mom and Dad don't have to worry. I paid for your university education. Before you say anything else, I wanted to do those things."

"Why did you come home?" Diego interrupted.

Jesse opened his mouth to shoot back an answer. But he chose to remain silent. A lot had been said with anger fueling the turmoil. He tried for a calmer approach, although his heartbeat thudded against his chest.

"I expected you to heal up and get back on the field before a younger version of you took your place," Diego pushed.

"Do *you* really want me to go?"

It was Diego's turn to be quiet.

"This is my home, too. I may not have been the best son. The best brother. But I never stopped being a part of this family." Jesse stood and headed for the door. "Circumstances have a way of charting our courses in life. When I got hurt, I wanted what was familiar around me. I wanted a neutral place." He opened the door. "There's no guarantee that I will stay here in Midway. But while I am here, I want us to be friends. We're already brothers." Jesse bowed his head. He didn't want to see his brother's anger. Now that he knew what the problem was, he had a decision to make. How far would he go to repair their relationship? Right now, he wasn't going to wait to find out. Now more than ever, he wanted to get home. That loneliness seemed like it would be more than a temporary condition.

Belinda hadn't stepped onto the floors of Meadows Media since her cousin had taken over. The place wasn't exactly her favorite hangout spot. Every year during her college years, she worked a summer internship. Afterward, a job was offered, but she turned it down. Nothing could drag her into Grace's world. Even now after she signed in at the security desk and got approval to head to the elevators, she wanted to turn and head for the exit.

Years may have dulled the humiliation, or so she kept telling herself. How many of her friends had a father who had embezzled from his mother-in-law's company? The full details didn't come out in the newspapers or in legal wrangling. Behind the scenes, the late-night meetings consisted of lawyers, her aunts and grandmother huddled in several private meetings. Sometimes her mother, Felicity, was included, but most times it was just Grace and the lawyers. Finally her father was given his deal. The details were never leaked, never gossiped about, not even discussed to this day by her mother.

Those days blurred one into the other. Belinda's volatile teenage emotions were laced heavily with anger, confession and ultimately the destruction of her parents' marriage. Her reality turned into a suffocating cocoon that enveloped her. She didn't know if the nightmare would consume her. Growing up, sometimes she wanted to disappear, put distance between the Meadows clan and herself. Who was she supposed to be loyal to—Grace, her mother, her father?

That big question had no answer. She wanted to please everyone and, at the same time, please no one. The family name always attracted those who wanted something for nothing. This was a motivating factor that propelled her to do her own thing and have her business.

Still, those niggling remnants of guilt had become a permanent part of her skin. The villain had been her father, Clifton Price. She could never replace what he'd taken—the hard cash or what he'd lost, which was everyone's respect and trust. Part of her wanted to come and work to earn back a smidgen of what he'd taken. The other part of her had wanted to run and hide from Grace, Meadows Media, even her cousins. But she wanted a fresh start, a place in time where Grace could look at her and not see her close resemblance to her father, where Belinda could not be judged for her father's sins. "Good morning, Miss Toussaint."

Belinda nodded to the employee who passed her with brisk energy of the highly motivated. Most of the employees knew the family members. Of course they would, when each family member's portrait lined the walls of the executive floor. For the blood relatives, their spot on the wall was permanent. For spouses, their place remained as long as the marriage was whole. Clifton, the villain, had been removed and after several years had been replaced with her stepfather's, Wade's, picture. Clifton was exiled not only from the company's walls, but from her life, when he closed off contact with her.

As she passed the glass-enclosed offices and the hive of cubicles, she couldn't help feeling glad that she didn't work there. Eight-plus hours in this environment would make her brain explode. Getting her physical-therapist certificate and working at various centers had provided experiences on the job that she wouldn't trade.

Stepping through the doors of the executive wing

was like entering another universe with her grandmother as the ruler over it all. She doubted that Dana had managed to shake the reverent atmosphere given it was only a few months since the official announcement that her cousin was Meadows Media's new CEO. She'd teased Dana to burn incense to cleanse the office and usher in her own vibe.

The office's professional ambiance was a major reason that any cousinly celebrations had taken place off the premises. Meet-ups were at each other's homes, mostly Belinda's, or on the rare occasions they dragged Belinda to a bar for happy hour.

"Hi, Miss Toussaint. Here to see Dana?" Sasha, the assistant, greeted her with an easy smile.

"Yep. Does she have time for her cousin?"

"One sec." Sasha got up and headed to the huge double doors that would open up to a space large enough for a small apartment.

Now that Belinda was here in the office, she did feel a bit nervous. Her problem was nothing compared to what Dana faced on a daily basis. But she missed hanging with her cousin and enjoying their lively chats. Since it was proving difficult for Dana to find time to meet up, she'd taken the deep breath and came on the pilgrimage to Meadows Media.

"You can go in," Sasha whispered. "She's got a meeting in ten minutes."

Belinda nodded. She approached the door and softly pulled it open. "Hey, there."

"Why are you acting as if you're walking into a church?" Dana hurried from around the desk and engulfed her in a bear hug. "Long time no see, stranger."

Though her cousin was the youngest of the cous-

ins, she wore maturity and top-level professionalism with class. Clearly, her navy blue suit that fit her
frame perfectly was custom-tailored. The matching
navy pumps shone with a killer heel that made her
wonder how Dana could deal with that constriction
for the entire day.

"I see you haven't redecorated." Belinda shifted
her admiring glance of her cousin's modern attire to
the office suite's fussy decor. Dark formal furniture
dominated the room. Heavy fabric drapes hung at
each window. The same chocolate-and-cream color
scheme from her childhood had remained in place.
"Please hurry up and liven up this place. You need
something Scandinavianish with lots of chrome and
glass."

"Shhh. I'm not concerned with redecorating. It's
expensive and unnecessary. Stop being disrespectful
to Grace's taste."

"Oh, my bad." Belinda genuflected and added an
eye roll to her mockery. "I can't believe you're here…
in this space. You're queen in charge and then some."
Belinda pushed down the swell of emotion. She wasn't
one to get teary-eyed. Memories of their childhood
together, her cousins also doubling as her best friends,
warmed her heart. "You know I'm proud of you."

Dana nodded. "Still feels good to hear it."

"Where's your sexy brown-skinned Brit?" Belinda
made a big production of looking for him around the
office, behind and under the desk, and finishing off
the search in her closet. "Wow! This is some walk-
in closet. Lucky I'm too tall to wear these clothes."
She brushed her hand along the pantsuits, skirt suits

and dresses that were neatly organized, while a large number of shoes filled the shoe cubbies.

"Get out of my closet. And Kent is on a quick trip to England. Back in two days." Her cousin still glowed with her new love.

"Miss him?"

"A whole lot." Dana's smile drooped. She glanced at the photograph on her desk.

"That's good. Means you're still in love."

"Of course!"

"Hey, I'm just checking in on matters of the heart. I'm making sure that I can still look forward to a serious announcement." Seeing her cousin relaxed and still confident in her relationship felt good.

"Stop rushing things. Is that why you're here? To give me grief?"

Belinda shook her head. "Nah, cuz. Needed your advice, ASAP."

"This is a first." Dana peered at her. When Belinda didn't say anything further, she pushed the button on her phone. "Sasha, reschedule my next appointment to later this afternoon. Then call Fiona and transfer her to my line, please."

"Are you quite done? Anyone else to call?" Belinda was used to the routine. The three cousins didn't breathe, move or do anything without one or all of them knowing. They took watching each other's back to a serious level.

"This must be really serious because you came all the way over here to see me." The phone rang and Dana quickly answered and pressed the speaker button. "Fiona, hey cuz. I've got Belinda in my office, laboring over some decision to be made."

Belinda deliberately dragged out her sing-song greeting. "Hey, Fiona, put down your case file and detective hat for a moment."

"How are you doing, Belinda?" Fiona asked in her characteristic husky voice.

Dana jumped in. "She needs an ear. Got time?"

"I'm at my desk, waiting for a call from the medical examiner. But go ahead. I'm sure we can solve the problem in minutes. If it was up to our dear Belinda, she'd drag out the solution over several lectures, cups of foreign herbal tea and the latest accomplishments with her horses." Only Fiona and Dana laughed.

"Look, I didn't come here to be the butt of your jokes." Their teasing didn't bother her. They were besties, after all. No, the problem was the growing urge to escape the office. Nerves over the surroundings and her current problem had her fidgeting and distracted.

"Okay, calm down. What's got a hold of your usual calm demeanor?" Dana's eyebrow cocked over a curious gaze.

"I fired someone today." Belinda heard their gasps. "It was necessary," she said in self-defense.

Dana patted her hand. "I'm sure it was. You go, girl. Don't tell me that I'm rubbing off on you."

"And don't tell me that you fired Tawny, your only employee," Fiona said. "I like her."

"It's not Tawny. It's Jesse." The man with haunting gray eyes, cool, alluring demeanor and wickedly sexy pair of lips.

"Who?" They sounded like owls.

"Santiago. Ed's son. Mr. Ex–Professional Soccer Player." And darn, if his body didn't look like he maintained its tiptop shape.

"Oh, now that's different. I like Ed, too," Fiona tossed out.

"Me, too," Dana added. "Plus, you know Grace absolutely adores him and Caroline, his wife. They were invited over for dinner a couple weeks ago."

"There's more. I'm also going to have to find a new contractor. With Jesse gone, I can't wait for Ed to get on his feet. Work on the riding ring has to begin immediately or the program won't start on time."

Silence.

Why wasn't this coming out with the sense of outrage that she'd felt earlier? Now that the emotional high had lowered with each passing hour, her complaint turned her response to an overreaction. That wasn't her style. But neither was Jesse…her style.

Dana sat back and folded her arms. "Now that you've made a mess of things, unnecessarily, I might add, what exactly do you want from us?"

"I don't feel good about it." Belinda usually didn't tend to second-guess herself. She arrived at her conclusions based on evidence, made her decisions and followed through the action. Give or take a few mistakes in judgment, overall, this system had worked in her life. And this morning, she'd been soaring over her smackdown because Jesse insulted her riding program, her horses, and acted too blasé about the job.

"You think…?" Dana pursed her mouth. "This is Ed's livelihood. You're not giving him a chance to come up with another solution. How will he feel that you tossed him off the job?" She leveled a ferocious stare. "You should have heard Ed talk about his retirement plans with Caroline. And then Grace and Grandpa Henry joined in, if you can imagine that. I hope that Kent and I are all goo-goo over each other when we get older." Dana's voice turned wistful.

"I'm not the bad guy." Belinda looked over at the phone for Fiona's support. Usually, they sided against Dana. Plus, Fiona wasn't wrapped up in any romantic fog. "Anyway, Ed's son was a complete jerk. That's not the word I really want to use. He acted as if rolling up his sleeves and doing a bit of work didn't meet his celebrity-athlete taste."

"Maybe he just wasn't cut out for customer service. More important, did he know his stuff?" Fiona finally rejoined the conversation. Her attention sounded as if it was being pulled from their group chat. That was not surprising, as she was a busy detective in a police precinct.

"Ed taught him or so he says." Belinda really didn't doubt that Ed would have shown his son the ropes.

"That's a good thing, if Ed trained him. That means he's darn good." Dana leaned forward. Curiosity lit up her eyes. "Did he make a pass at you?" The smirk gave away any true concern for her cousin if he really had.

"No."

"Are you mad that he didn't?" Fiona asked.

"Oh, my gosh, would both of you get past the high school stuff?" Fact: he did check her out. Fact: he didn't take the job seriously. Fact: he didn't fight to stick around.

"What made you fire him? Something illegal? I can check to see if he's got a record, celebrity or not." Trust Fiona to be ready to use her detective skills.

"He didn't want to work. Pretty much said so. Complained and whined about the smell of my horses."

Fiona laughed and then Dana joined in.

Belinda fumed. "I love my horses."

"That doesn't mean that they don't smell." Dana raised her arm to ward off Belinda's verbal attack. "I love your horses. I just know how it may seem to someone for the first time."

"It's not as if I hid what the job was." Belinda felt herself getting worked up all over again.

"Was he a good soccer player? I'm more curious about why he's home. And to play at carpentry is a bit suspect, don't you think, Dana?" Fiona's mind had drifted off course. "Maybe I *should* check into his background."

"So unnecessary. He's not a criminal." Belinda's hot defense of Jesse shocked herself. "And frankly I don't care why he's not playing anymore. I need my riding ring built." Belinda didn't doubt that Fiona could find a file that encompassed Jesse's life from birth to his diss toward her company. But they'd never spied on each other or on the romantic prospects that wandered into their lives. And she didn't want to start that practice with Jesse, despite her desire to clobber him over the head.

"What do you want to do?" Dana waited.

"I'm having second thoughts." Belinda threw her head back on the chair and blew out a long sigh. "I feel as I'm coming out at the losing end of this."

Dana prompted, "Why did he get under your skin so much? Yeah, he sounds like a jerk. But you aren't looking for a soul mate. You need a reputable person to come in, do the job. When it's over, he'll be on his way."

"Yeah, pretty much." Dana was right. Jesse San-

tiago was a pompous jackass. On the flip side, maybe
he could wield a hammer like a pro.

"Take a chill pill. Blame your hasty decision on the
stress, and get Jesse back on your team."

Belinda followed the logic. Still, the path to the
solution grated. "It's going to kill me to apologize."

"You're the CEO of your company. Think like
one." Fiona echoed Dana's argument. "You've got
plans that are bigger than Jesse. All you need him
for is to nail pieces of wood together. As long as he's
respectful, then don't sweat the small stuff. You're a
tough woman. I know you won't take any crap from
him."

"Did you call Ed? Please tell me that you didn't."
Dana pulled her attention.

"Not yet." The enormity of this situation taking off
in another direction, if Ed found out, hit her. What if
Jesse told on her? Her diplomatic relations would be
put to the test without that added issue.

"Good." Dana leaned over and patted her hand.
"Don't panic. That's the best thing that you could have
delayed doing. Ed never has to know that you were
willing to kick his son off the project."

"And Grace doesn't have to know that you messed
with her favorite contractor," Fiona reminded.

Belinda couldn't agree more. "Grandma came to
visit. Felt like more of a business appointment. The
usual discussion—wants me to work here."

Fiona burst in before Dana could hide her shock.
"Oh, damn, please don't let her come knocking on
my door."

"You've got a real job." Belinda leaned over the
phone. "I'm the one that is around seemingly mess-

ing with the touchy-feely job that she probably considers a waste of time."

"I like your touchy-feely business," Dana stated. "You're a thoughtful person. And I'm sure Grace doesn't feel so harshly about what you're doing. She was there when you received certification to be an equine-therapy specialist. She also showed up when you bought your first horse. That was a big deal to see her there."

"And she did it for you, Belinda," Fiona added.

Having Grace show an interest in her pursuits did provide that additional boost in deciding to start her business. Her entire family knew the real motivation behind Dreamweaver Riding Program—Maritza Carnegie. They understood the pain and emotional distress of emerging unscathed from the car accident; meanwhile, her best friend suffered a spinal cord injury. What they couldn't deal with was how long she'd been torn over a friendship that unfortunately had dissolved soon after the accident. The ordeal almost broke her emotionally.

Regardless of the chasm born of anger and remorse over Maritza's accident, Belinda hoped that one day she could repair the emotional damage. One way to do so was with the riding program. After witnessing her friend's rehabilitation from afar and talking with her therapists, the idea to create Dreamweaver formed and took hold. She started on a small scale with two horses. In order to take it to the next level, she needed renovations and more funding. Even after fixing the issue with Jesse, there was still the matter of raising funds and holding on to the other donors.

She'd do anything to keep her dream alive.

"Maybe I *should* work here." Belinda imagined that she must be having an out-of-body experience for those words to spill from her.

"What?" Dana snapped forward and pushed up Belinda's chin until they were locked in a direct stare with each other. "Why? Not that I wouldn't love to have you work here. But you're giving me whiplash."

"I lost a donor yesterday. And I don't think it will be the last. I barely make a living anyway. The last time I rented out some of my extra rooms to grad students, that ended in court." Belinda took a deep breath. "That's why I think that I should take a job at Meadows. It's an annoying thought that buzzes around in my head every time something goes screwy. I just didn't want it to be at Grace's say-so."

"I know that feeling." Fiona certainly had had her life shaped at Grace's hands. Her mother, Verona, had been a wild child and was only eventually reined in by a respectable marriage to an appropriate connection. "Ladies, I have to run. Got to go solve a crime and hopefully make an arrest."

"Stay safe," Dana said.

"Love you," Belinda chimed in before Fiona ended the call.

Belinda stretched and looked over at Dana, the youngest and the most ambitious of the cousins. Success and she had been close partners from high school onward. Even after her rise up the ladder in Meadows, with all the pressures of taking over from Grace, she slipped on the CEO jacket with style and skill. All her detractors had to pause in their criticism as the company pushed onward with plans to venture into uncharted waters. Jealousy or envy didn't cloud their relationship at all. But she did wish that she also could feel one hundred percent sure of her path, to feel that sense of satisfaction that she'd turned a dream into her passion.

That skill belonged to Fiona, the detective who worked around the clock, filling her life with hours going after the bad guys and girls. She lived the farthest away and only joined in on holidays and maybe on family gatherings. A lot of Grace's manipulations with Fiona's mother had set the tone of her arm's length relationship with the family. Even her grandmother didn't push Fiona or hint that she should work at Meadows. And like all of them, she could certainly have any job, including that of head of security. As large and profitable as the company had become, the crackpot threats and harassment had also increased against Grace and now Dana. If Dana really needed Fiona on staff, her cousin would answer the call. Otherwise, Fiona would continue doing her job as a detective in the Rochester Missing Persons Division. The only person she'd answer to was Dana or Belinda herself.

"I'm kicking around an idea." Dana said, her voice hesitant.

Belinda waited, not sure what shade of crazy Dana was going to propose.

"What if you worked for Kent?"

"Kent? Your boyfriend?"

"Yep. He needs an assistant as he plans to expand here in America. Right now, he's using a temping service. But I think it would be ideal. It's not a full day of work, but it's something. And he needs someone flexible and trustworthy. For your part, you need some dollars."

Belinda turned over the possibility in her mind. A sliver of light cracked through her unhappiness.

"You can plan your day with that deal." Dana pointed toward the door. "Coming here to work, you know that you won't be able to do anything else in your day. Our employees bleed the colors of Meadows. They spout the company's motto. Working nine-to-five is for interns."

"Gosh, you sound like a boss. That spiel is for regular folk who come through the Meadows Media doors. But you're talking to me." Belinda rolled her eyes. "You sound like a bully."

Dana ignored her comment. "Just say the word, and I'll talk to Kent."

"One thing at a time. Let me fix the Santiago thing and then I'll get back to you on working for Kent." Belinda hoped that she would get a double win on the two items. "Don't blindside Kent by having me pop up in his office. Let him decide if he wants to work with me. And my feelings wouldn't be hurt if he doesn't want to go this route. Heck, he might have his own plan. Ever thought of that?"

"Yeah, well, *my* feelings would be hurt." Dana winked. "Plus it will have been over a week since I last saw him. I'm pretty sure that I can get anything I want from him…in between sessions."

"TMI." Belinda pressed the heels of her palms against her ears. "And on that note, I'm outta here."

Dana chuckled. "Seriously, though, don't let pride screw you over. And don't worry about the donor.

We'll plan a big bash, a fund-raising drive for your company."

"No way."

"Yes, way. Grace had her pet charities. I'm developing mine."

"Don't you have to get permission?"

"Let me show you how it's done." Dana dialed the phone.

Belinda took a deep breath.

"Hi, Sasha. Could you come in, please?"

Belinda didn't know what to expect. As she turned to the door that opened, Sasha walked in, looking between her and Dana. Her questioning gaze intensified as she got closer.

"In two to three months, I'd like to have a fund-raiser for Belinda's organization. What is my calendar looking like?"

Sasha tapped the iPad screen and expanded the screen. "You don't have any openings."

"Dana, I don't want you to rush into anything." Belinda knew her cousin would do anything for her. But this wasn't a small favor.

"Clear one of those weekends. My cousins Fiona and Belinda will be hosting the fund-raiser."

"Fiona?" Oh, now her cousin just might use her gun on her. She hated to be blindsided.

"Not a problem." Sasha typed whatever she needed to on to the screen.

"I want you to take the lead, too. We can sit down and discuss. Or do it by conference call. It might be like pulling teeth to get Fiona in here."

"You ain't kiddin'." Belinda didn't know who would be the one to break it to her. Maybe Sasha?

"I will talk to Fiona after you all tell her what you've volunteered her to do." Sasha tapped the screen. "Is that it?"

"Yes, that's it." Dana barely contained her grin.

"Not even funny." Belinda was still amazed that Sasha seemed to be the one running the office. "But appreciated."

"Good. Well, I really do have to get back to work. And I want you to stop worrying so you can go do what needs to be done."

Belinda nodded. The heavy weight that pressed on her shoulders when she arrived at the office had eased up. Talking through her problems with her cousins, coming up with options and coming to terms with what she needed to do with Jesse—it all helped lift the veil of depression.

At the top of the priorities list was making amends with Jesse. But if he threw that cocky behavior at her, he would live to regret it. As soon as she got back, she wasn't going to delay what needed to be done. Mr. Sexpot and she could have a second chance.

Chapter 5

Belinda was back in her car, feeling one hundred percent better. She turned up the volume of her favorite Jill Scott CD and sang along. Her morning took a brighter and happier turn. All she had to do was follow the plan. She pushed on her earpiece and dialed her office. "Hey, Tawny, any messages?"

"Nope. Where are you?"

"I headed over to Dana's. Had to take care of stuff. But I'm returning to the office. What's the calendar looking like?"

"No one's coming today. But tomorrow you have a few more potential clients. Then later today you have an interview with the county newspaper."

"I hear your warning. In other words, don't go off the radar."

"Uh-huh." Tawny knew her so well.

"What about emails? Hoping that Ed hadn't gotten wind of the firing."

"About that…"

"Yeah?" Dread immediately crept into Belinda's belly. Her fingers tightened their curl around the steering wheel.

Tawny's voice lowered. "Um…you've got a visitor. He's waiting to see you. Says it's important that he talks to you, today."

"Who?" Belinda hated when Tawny dragged out good info.

"Jesse."

"Get outta here. In my office?" Belinda was glad the traffic light switched to red. The shockwaves of surprise almost rendered her motionless. *He came back*.

"Well, right now, he's not in your office. He's at the stable."

"Did he say what he wants?" At the stable? That had been one of the points of their conflict. Was he trying to make a point?

"All he kept saying was that it was an emergency. He needed to talk to you right away."

"Does he look pissed off? Or does he look like he has iced water in the veins, like the way he did yesterday after I fired him?"

"More like stoic. Quiet. Intense. Wasn't flirty. And definitely wasn't cocky."

This was definitely an interesting turn of events. "Tell him to meet me at Barney's. And could you make a reservation, please? I'll be there in fifteen minutes. Oh, push the interview off to tomorrow. Then you can head home, since nothing's happening."

"Then I won't know what he wanted. What you said. What y'all did." Tawny groaned her protest.

"That'll give you incentive to come to work to-morrow."

"You're cruel. But I'll pass on the message and then lock up," Tawny replied. "Maybe I can beat the forecasted storm."

"Take it easy. See you tomorrow." Belinda discon-nected the call.

So, Jesse had returned. Why? Was he bringing a message from Ed? At least he was alone and not with a lawyer to discuss contract terms. Hopefully, the sit-uation didn't have to escalate to that level.

Over a meal and a couple drinks, she might be able to convince Jesse to remain on the job. Now all she needed was for him to play nice and say yes, without realizing that she was pretty close to begging. The project wasn't going to be a long-term one. Maybe they could put aside their misgivings and proceed ahead for the short duration. She could teach him a thing or two about normal life. He could share the glossy details of the superstar life. Somewhere in be-tween, they could find common ground to tolerate each other.

"Time to eat some humble pie," she confessed to Jill Scott as the singer continued to belt out another song. Turning up the volume, she blasted the music as a soundtrack to the drive on the other side of town.

Barney's Bar and Grill was one of the newer es-tablishments that Jesse had encountered on his return home. The place was quiet on the weekdays. Once Thursday afternoon hit, through to the early dinner crowd on Sunday, the parking lot stayed packed. Even the side streets off the main road had to take the overflow traffic. Thankfully today, he didn't have that problem with the impromptu meeting with Belinda, which took place between the lunch and dinner hours. With the switch in venue, he had to apologize in a public setting. Too bad it wasn't a normal meal between friends. He'd much rather spend an hour sipping on beer, getting to know Belinda.

"Good afternoon, sir. Welcome to Barney's. How many in your party?"

Jesse shook his head at the hostess who reached for the menu. "I'm meeting someone. Belinda Toussaint."

"Right behind you."

Her greeting stroked him like a warm gentle hand over the length of his arm. His shoulder actually twitched. "Oh, I didn't expect…" Not sure what he had been supposed to expect. Maybe that she was already here, which she was, and he'd make the walk of shame alone to her table. That she wouldn't be only inches away from him, close enough to smell her perfume, close enough to see the double ear piercing on her left lobe, close enough to reach over and pull the hair fastener around her ponytail. Jesse took a step back to kill any sudden impulses.

"I should have reservations, but I'm cancelling." Belinda had taken the lead and approached the hostess. She'd barely looked at him.

The hostess looked alarmed. Her attention shifted to him as if he should correct the situation. Unfortunately, he had his own problems to solve. All he could offer was an apologetic shrug.

Belinda continued explaining to the hostess. "It's

my fault. An emergency meeting came up. Sorry for the inconvenience."

Jesse didn't know what the heck was going on. So far, he was bouncing from place to place at Belinda's command. Like the hostess, he was disappointed that he wasn't getting the chance to fix the issue. Unlike the hostess, he masked it with a cool reserve and pretended not to be irritated.

"Let's take my car." She'd breezed past him. Once again, a mere glance tossed in his direction. With her latest command, she'd swept out the restaurant as if a queen. If she kept this behavior up, he'd have a hard time remembering his apology.

"Where are we going?" Jesse slowed and then stopped.

"What?" She finally realized that he wasn't following. "I said we'll take my car."

"I heard you." Jesse remained stubbornly in place. "Where are we going? I only came to talk to you." And to see her again, but not like a puppy following her.

"You're right. My brain was moving faster than my words. Are you free for the afternoon?"

He nodded. To spend the afternoon with her—hell, yeah.

"Good. It's a surprise." When he raised his brows, she hastily continued through a wide grin, "I promise…it's not bad."

Jesse didn't like being laughed at. Even if Belinda's laughter had a rich rippling sound that shot out and hovered before falling around him.

"You need to stop with the suspicious vibe. I promise to bring you back, safe and sound."

"Uh-huh." Jesse resumed walking. "I will follow you in my car." Taking back some control was his top priority.

"Yes, you can. But I want to talk to you." Before he reached her, she took off at the brisk pace across the parking lot to her shiny black SUV. She looked at him over the hood. "I suspect you may want to talk to me, also."

"No argument, there." Talk. Hug. Kiss. Yeah, there was a whole lot that he might want to do. The familiar warm rush pumped through his belly to his groin. Should he drive or submit to her wish and the temptation defining his thoughts? A fat, warm raindrop hit his nose, followed by another. *Decision made.* He opened the passenger door and hopped in just in time, as the clouds released their water in a deluge.

Within seconds, a fast-moving storm rolled in with dark thunder clouds and a formidable display of blue-silver streaks of lightning. Rain pounded the area, including the SUV. Wiper blades whipped aside the water from the windshield, giving him spotty views of the surroundings. The blurred images of trees and neighborhoods didn't provide any clues as to their destination. Belinda hadn't stopped singing since they started their journey. From the widening distance between neighborhoods, he suspected that they were heading into farm country.

Reading signs into everything wasn't in his belief system. Normally. Nothing had an air of the normal or of the regular around her. Every thunderclap felt like an exclamation point to the time he spent with Belinda, past, present and hopefully, future.

His driver kept her foot on the gas and her focus

on their destination in parts unknown. Hopefully, the turn in the weather wasn't a signal of how his apology would be taken. From the occasional side-glances of her profile, he couldn't tell if this would be a good meeting or not. And if she didn't stop singing and acting as though they were on a Sunday afternoon drive, he'd muzzle her.

Jesse turned his attention out the window. The gray, rain-soaked landscape sliding past his window had a hypnotic effect on the worrisome thoughts pinging in his head. Another thunderclap set his teeth on edge. He glanced over to Belinda. She'd stopped singing. Whatever internal dialogue she was having, her demeanor spoke volumes. Her mouth had a grim set. As a result, tension between them swirled with a growing edge of something about to touch off.

The silence now bothered him. What to say to dispel the quiet? It wasn't as though they had a winning streak and could rehash the highlights. If they'd had a successful meeting, they'd now be chatting about the work schedule, the materials and what was behind her vision. As he'd learned, anything dealing with her vision had to be approached on tiptoe.

"Are we almost there?" he asked after forty-five minutes of them navigating nonstop rolling hills and winding roads. "Are we in the state?"

"Just about there." Her face relaxed for a small smile. "Yes, you're still in New York."

"Good. Needed to know if I had to send out an SOS."

"Afraid that I'd kidnap you?"

"Nah. Maybe you were lost and refused to use your GPS."

"Think I'm stubborn?" She glanced over at him with a smile.

"Better than me thinking that you secretly planned to kidnap me." Jesse had no problems with the kidnap option or the driving blind in small-town America. Not when the experience came with Belinda playing a prominent role.

"All my kidnappings are done by Tawny. She's much more unsympathetic to any cries of help." Now Belinda was grinning. The idea clearly humored her.

"I'll take that under advisement if I cross paths with Tawny."

The conversation dipped. This time, the mood had lightened considerably. Jesse didn't mind the comfortable pause.

"So…is there a girlfriend waiting impatiently for you back home?"

The question caught him off guard, but he readily replied, "No. Not at all." He looked over at her. "Anyone for you?"

She shook her head. "Not for a while." Belinda looked at him, up and down, and stared hard at his face. "And I like it that way."

"I didn't argue." Jesse agreed with the last emphatic sentiment, but her adamant tone nettled him. Plus, she had blindsided him, a frequent occurrence, with the very personal turn to their exchange.

"A man would interfere with my plans."

"You have to lay down the law at the beginning. Kind of like a policy and procedures."

She shrugged. "Most guys think they can change me. They agree to the terms and then turn into bullies."

Jesse heard the still-fresh anger and weary disappointment. "Some women think they can change the man after the seduction is over. It turns into a project like spring cleaning."

She sucked her teeth and glared at him.

He teased, "You didn't want to hear the other side of the same issue?"

"Not really. And I doubt any girlfriends changed a hair on your head."

"I'm stubborn like that." Jesse could now admit that none of the women had stood a chance against his soccer career. They'd lost the battle before it had really begun.

"You sound proud of that trait."

"And you're proud of your independence." He stated the obvious and admired her for it.

"Yeah, very much so."

"Looks like we found one thing that we can agree on."

"Hmm." The corner of her mouth tilted upward.

"A first step," Jesse declared. He liked the direction where they were headed. Settling deeper into the seat, he relaxed considerably. "Music?" His hand hovered over the radio dial.

She nodded.

He pushed in the power-on button, wondering what stations were on her top list. A soft jazz played before a singer's soulful voice pushed away the tension. Not an expert on the top jazz singers, he didn't have a clue who sang, but enjoyed it nevertheless. While Belinda continued with the quiet spell, Jesse sat back, tapping his fingers to the snappy beats, while looking out the rain-splattered window. When it was quiet like this, there was nothing to distract him from the soft scent of her perfume. It was a subtle mix that seductively issued an invitation for him to investigate the landing spots where the fragrance connected to her skin.

A glance to his left revealed her chewing on her bottom lip. At least he wasn't the only one suffering a case of the jitters. The constant movement of her mouth looked in need of a sedating touch along the pillowy curved bow. His hand twitched for the volunteer duty. And that's what friends, intimate ones, who could read each other's signals, would do. But that wasn't the case here. The fact did disappoint. He doubted they would ever hit that upward slope to friendship, much less anything further.

The rain finally eased to a soft mist. After their hour-and-a-half trek from city life and outlet malls, they had a long stretch of road to seemingly nowhere in front of them. A few horse and rider caution signs lined the road. Jesse heard the signal click on. Apparently they were turning right. A large brown sign came into view but too quickly for him to read. From the smooth asphalt, they turned onto a rocky dirt road that jostled them within an inch of their lives in the SUV.

"Is this still the surprise? Or did you change your mind about kidnapping me?" Jesse had had enough of the ride-along.

"We're here."

Immediately after Belinda's announcement, the narrow drive lined with large trees opened up to acres of cleared land.

Jesse looked at the oversize archway with designs of galloping horses over an official entrance. Each bounce of the car had him gripping the door handle. He actually looked forward to getting out and placing his feet on unmoving ground. Compared to Belinda's driving, his style would be a senior citizen on a Sunday drive. His teeth clicked together on the final bounce, as she stopped and put the car in Park.

"This is Sunny Dale Riding Club."

Jesse peered out the window and swept his gaze over the width of the perimeter. A large stable with an enclosed riding ring took up most of the front area. Small buildings and a barn were on the far left. No one was in sight. In the distance, to the right, was a country home with its white picket fence. He noticed cars parked in front of the property. Still, all was quiet. Too quiet.

"It's an assisted riding program for children with special needs." Belinda opened the door and hopped out.

Jesse remained in place. Not only was he stiff from the long ride, but he was cautious about why they were at this place. Why did he need to be here?

She faced him with her hands on her hips. He read her lips and got out of the SUV. Once again, she seemed to be laughing at him. He had to laugh at his own reluctance before he hopped out.

"You know, if I didn't see any signs of life, I would have done a dive roll."

"Are you always this suspicious?"

"When a beautiful woman tells me to jump in her car and takes off for parts unknown…yeah, I'm suspicious." He joined her. "For the record, I don't like surprises," he warned. Especially when the blindsiding promised to be an experience that poked at his heart and wound itself around his emotions.

"Shh. Soak it in."

Jesse's eyebrow popped up. What nirvana experience was she having? He wasn't going to close his eyes. And he wasn't going to lean back, close his eyes and inhale. While his nervousness held him back, it allowed him to openly observe Belinda for a few seconds. With her arms flung open as if she was on a mountaintop ready to belt out songs in a movie musical, her breasts were thrust up like delicious treats on a platter. Thinking that he'd have to snap his fingers in Belinda's face to bring her back to earth, Jesse was glad to see the place suddenly come to life. The sudden appearance of people from various buildings felt like the beginning of a scaled-down flash mob. Maybe the change in the weather returned them to their activities. He took the opportunity to turn away and walked off the hard bulge that was damned inappropriate.

"Hey, wait up." This time, it was Belinda hurrying to catch up with him.

"Figured I'd leave you to commune with nature."

"You should really take time to pause and enjoy life," she admonished.

"I'm definitely pausing. Not sure about the enjoyment part."

"Well, let's see what we can do about that." She slipped her arm through his and he almost tripped over a rock.

"Let's not," he muttered, struggling against the desire to cover her hand, resting at the crook of his elbow, with his hand. This stroll was definitely not casual. His throat suddenly felt parched because the rest of his body had suddenly heated.

Clueless to what she was doing to him, Belinda pointed out, "The ones in the green shirts and khaki pants are the employees."

The uniformed workers emerged from the buildings, chatting and goofing around. A handler holding the reins led a horse with its rider, who looked no more than ten years old, from the stable. The slow walk brought the trio closer to where Belinda and Jesse had paused to let them pass.

"That horse is huge. Should that child be on there?" Jesse blurted. His last recollection of being this close to a horse was at a carnival for the pony rides. He'd gotten close and decided that it wasn't worth it. The horse had snorted at him and shifted its weight. One look at the hooves and he'd doubled down on his decision.

"The horse is trained for this. Although the child might be nervous, they are introduced to each other gradually."

The handler kept a close eye on the child. And so did Jesse. He didn't consider himself hero material, but he'd be willing to make a save if necessary.

On his face, the young boy wore a mix of nervousness and occasional bursts of sheer joy that erupted into hearty giggles. His attention stayed glued on the back of the horse with quick shifts of his eyes to the handler when she softly instructed him. They entered the riding ring.

Only then did he and Belinda move toward the fence to continue watching. Belinda no longer held his arm. She was enraptured with the trio's measured progress around the ring. "See how the counselor communicates with the horse and the child."

Jesse nodded. It was amazing how gently the horse walked, as if aware how important it was for its rider to be confident.

"Patience and reinforcement are needed."

When the handler raised her hand for a high five, Jesse wanted in on the celebration. The boy looked over at them. Jesse offered a thumbs-up. The boy grinned, answering with his own thumbs-up.

"That's nice of you," Belinda remarked.

"He did a good job, that's all." Jesse had to admit that this child and his progress had snagged his attention. He cared. That didn't bother him, except the swiftness to that destination point.

"There's another riding ring on the farther side. Let's go take a look."

Jesse didn't resist. He wanted to see more of the program. Nothing around here was from his world— horses, the rural outdoors and more horses. Here, hope was the powerful motivator. He imagined every visit and hour these children spent on conditioning or strengthening therapy with the horses was a step on a long emotional journey.

"What are you thinking?"

"I'm impressed."

"The first time that I saw the program, I was moved, too." She paused. "I'm always amazed."

Jesse heard the hitch in her voice. "I had no idea of places like this. I guess I never had to know."

"Yes, usually something personal or tragic makes us aware."

Jesse understood that more than ever. Diego's accusation had burrowed deep in his conscience. Only his injury had brought him home. The experience also opened his eyes to what he'd missed while being away, but also the pain he'd caused because of his decisions. Everyone needed a haven for their souls to heal.

He took a step back, unused to the trickle of questioning emotions that threatened to grow into a swell. Uncomfortable with the depth of his feelings, he blew out an exasperated breath.

"Why are we here? I get whatever point you're trying to make."

"Bear with me. I'm not playing games, not playing with emotions."

"You're about to teach me a lesson," Jesse summarized. No matter how attractive and fierce Belinda Toussaint was, this mind game was screwing with him. And he didn't like it one bit.

"Life is one big classroom," she remarked.

"Now she's quoting like a guru." He accepted the hard nudge to his arm.

"Good afternoon, welcome to Sunny Dale," a woman greeted. Wide, friendly smiles welcomed them as they approached. She was one half of a middle-aged couple who'd come out from a nearby building. They were not in the green-and-khaki uniform worn by the employees. Instead, they were dressed casually, but their combined demeanor said they were in charge.

"Hi." Jesse responded first, since the woman focused on him.

He noticed that the couple had their arms securely around each other's waist.

"Isabella. Dimitri. Good to see you again." Belinda stepped in with her greeting.

"Belinda, my dear," Isabella responded.

Jesse watched the dramatic hug and kiss on each cheek. His shoulder tensed when Dimitri added an extra kiss and then slid his hands up and down Belinda's arms. The three were definitely friends. And their quick catch-up on each other's health and well-being left him as the odd one out.

"This is Jesse Santiago," Belinda introduced him. "I wanted him to see firsthand what a therapeutic riding program looked like. Converting the masses, one person at a time."

He nodded, not sure why he had to meet these people. No conversion was necessary. He didn't have to be swayed to do the job.

"I was worried about the rainstorm, that you wouldn't have been able to walk the grounds and get a full experience of the place." Isabella motioned for them to follow her to the stable. "You also came at a good time because we have two teens in the middle of their sessions."

"Jesse and I were admiring the two kids in the riding ring."

Belinda made it sound like they were a couple. Of course, it could be that he wanted them to be a couple. If that was the case in his fantasy, he wouldn't pick this place as the first date. He'd want to spend the time in a cozy setting, staring into her eyes, sharing only the best parts of himself.

From behind, Dimitri leaned in between Jesse's and Belinda's faces. "Doing this will change your lives. It does help to have each other because it will be a lot of work. We were worried when it seemed like this was a project that you were going to do on your own."

Jesse didn't want to be the one to pop the balloon that he wasn't with Belinda. And he had no idea what they were all talking about.

"It's still just me," Belinda clarified. "These are my mentors," she explained to Jesse.

"Oh." Isabella's look accused him of falling short.

"Can you give us a minute?" Belinda raised a finger in the air. Silence descended.

The couple moved off to tend to one of their horses.

Jesse couldn't take it any longer. "What's going on? I feel as though I'm on a field trip…involuntarily. Not that your company is unpleasant." He exhaled. "But all of this feels a bit over the top." He looked over his shoulder at Isabella and Dimitri. "And they feel like time-share salespeople." He folded his arms and stared off at the corner of the room.

"Shh. They are kindhearted. Flamboyant, maybe." She stepped into his line of vision. "They've helped me every step of the way, once that initial spark of the idea formed. When Tawny said that you were in the office, I had no plans other than to meet you and talk." She mirrored his folded arms stance. "Then I had a change of heart. I figured you'd be game, long enough for me to bring you here." She relaxed her arms. "I wanted to show you a thriving horse-assisted therapy program because this is what I want to re-create on a smaller scale. Baby steps, you know. You see, I don't think that you understood what I was doing. What I'm trying to create."

"Why does that matter? Why do I have to under-

stand? I agree that it's noble—you'll get no argument
from me." Jesse didn't share that his father had given
him no real insight on what Belinda wanted to accomplish. When he arrived on site, he'd expected reports
about damage on the roof, maybe a wall that had rot-
ted and needed fresh planks. Nothing close to what he
was seeing here. "Why would you want to do this?"

"Still judging me?"

He shook his head, then slowly nodded. "Yeah, I
guess I am. You've got Meadows Media as a primary
career choice… Sorry." His hand grazed her cheek to
accompany the apology.

But Belinda shrugged away from his apology and
touch. Her mouth tightened into a straight line full of
disapproval. Her shoulders were squared, rigid ready
for a fight; her dark brown eyes were squinted tightly,
their laser-like precision targeting him.

"Maritza Carnegie is why I'm doing this. She is
a dear friend whose injuries required additional care
after the surgeries. What she endured inspired me to
become a physical therapist. Then I read about the
increased research on, and documented benefits of,
equine therapy. So I decided to continue with this
avenue of rehabilitation. In a nutshell, that's why I'm
doing this."

Once again, he'd pissed her off. Yet all he wanted
to do was to kiss those full soft lips until he melted
away her anger.

"Dimitri, Isabella, we're ready." Belinda's upbeat
voice didn't match her cold regard for him.

He stepped aside as she joined the weirdly happy
couple. They certainly lucked out with Belinda's
breezy smile and warmhearted small talk. On the

other hand, his attempts to be friendly kept getting him stuck in solitary confinement. Damn it. He never had a problem casting his own spell on women, showing them a good time, having himself a good time. Why couldn't it be easy with this woman? Why was she different?

"I know that I can sound like a jackass," he leaned in and whispered.

Her head turn practically snapped at his comment. Her mouth opened, but nothing came out. He considered that a blessing since she wasn't going to be complimenting him. Her obvious shock distracted her enough for her to stumble. He reached out to steady her. His hand lingered longer than necessary on her hip. He wanted to pull her back toward him. Wanted to press his pelvis against her backside. Instead, he slowly dropped his hand and let his heart pound out the adrenaline rush.

He continued whispering in her ear as they walked behind the couple who were explaining every detail and nook of the stable. "I wasn't knocking the project. Just trying to understand why."

"Does it matter?"

"The whys always matter. Disclosure is like opening a window to the soul." Jesse let her be and stepped up toward Dimitri and Isabella to listen to their presentation. He glanced at her. She watched him with a guarded look. Maybe Belinda had her private reasons and ambitions.

"Through this door, we will head into the stables. Here are our horses. We have eight, but only four are used with clients." Isabella stepped aside, while Dimitri held open the door for their entrance.

"The other horses?" Jesse entered the stable with the group. Yep, the horse smell that he'd complained about hit his nostrils. No one else seemed to mind.

"The other horses are used for grooming and tending exercises. Not every client can physically ride. Some may be too afraid to deal with these beautiful creatures." Isabella stroked the nose of a horse that poked its head out for attention.

"Are the horses trained here?" Jesse continued walking through the stable. His expertise on horses stalled at zero.

The horses were indeed beautiful creatures with coats that shone under the natural light. As the four of them walked between the stalls, the horses dropped their heads and then flipped their noses up. Isabella made kissing sounds which excited them and resulted in more head tosses. As she talked and stroked their jaws, the horses responded with definite interest.

Dimitri opened one of the stalls and walked in to where a large, jet-black horse overwhelmed the space. The horse curled its upper lip.

"Not to worry," Dimitri remarked. "Thunder is happy to see us."

The horse not only flipped its head, but stamped the ground and moved sideways. Not once did Dimitri react. Meanwhile, Jesse had stepped back, ready for a stampede. All around him, the other horses seemed to feed off Thunder's energy. It felt like playtime in the stalls. Horses whinnied. Their hooves tapped out a chaotic rhythm until Dimitri exited the stall.

Jesse had to admit that he was also impressed with the children who weren't intimidated by these large animals. As he passed the horses, he wanted to follow the urge to touch them. Hesitantly, he walked closer to the stall, praying they wouldn't go wild and force a breakout. His imagination wouldn't stop. Too many childhood fears took hold.

"Have you had a bad experience with a horse?" Isabella asked. She continued with kissing sounds to a horse that wiggled its top lip, as if it wanted to chat and laugh.

"No. I just don't like that they have a mind of their own." He did have that urge to stroke the long, graceful necks of the horses, like his companions did.

"Those aren't the only things he doesn't like with a mind of their own." Belinda played with a horse next to him. "Women are at the top of the list."

Dimitri laughed heartily, causing the horses to paw nervously at the ground. "Are you one of those men who has to feel in control?"

"Definitely not answering." Jesse reached a tentative finger to the horse.

"You men always have to feel like you're in control with something between the legs." Isabella smacked her husband's head with a playful swat. They exited the other side of the building. "I hope that you don't let your fear overtake the pleasure of riding. When you're riding, you forget all your problems."

"At some point, though, you do have to stop riding. And the problems are all there waiting for you." Jesse felt Belinda's poke in his ribs.

"Yes. But for those precious long minutes, you will feel unburdened. Don't you agree, Belinda? You're an accomplished rider yourself."

Once again, Jesse pictured Belinda in a form-enhancing outfit. Although she would look sexy as hell sitting proudly on any horse, she would also be suitably sexy wearing such an outfit in his bed.

"Horseback riding is like joining my spirit with my horse. Out there, riding the trail, we're both enjoying the freedom to just be, living intensely in the present, the moment. Although I ride alone, I never feel alone when I'm on my horse. We strengthen our partnership for that short hour of riding. I can be... me." Her voice slowly dropped to a husky whisper.

"Well, maybe...one day." Jesse tossed out the weak offer. With his schedule and responsibility, he couldn't picture himself riding around in the fields. But he did learn not to judge those who obviously found joy with their four-legged friends.

"Belinda, don't let him live with this fear," Dimitri teased. "You have to man up." He playfully punched Jesse's arm with his thick fist. "Now we'll go to the rehab facility."

Isabella took the lead. "We have physical therapists and play areas for the clients. We really don't want them to feel as though it is all work. Improvements on motor skills occur with the simpler games. Belinda, this wasn't complete when you came to see the place."

"This is amazing," Belinda remarked. Again, that happiness lit up her face. The smile that made rare appearances opened up, enhancing her beauty.

He had to agree, though. The rehab facility was impressive with its open floor plan. Exercise equipment for people with various physical limitations filled the room. An indoor pool occupied the other half of the building. Several kids and individual coaches were in the pool. Soft music played overhead.

"The kids pick their music."

Jesse liked the atmosphere.

"Let's move on, shall we?" Isabella ushered them out of the building. "Next door is a cafeteria. As you can see, there isn't much out here. The children are brought here for most of the day. We also have a sleeping area if anyone needs to rest."

"You've thought of everything," Belinda remarked. She strolled ahead, inspecting the various perks that Isabella mentioned.

Dimitri tapped Jesse on the arm. "It took time. We started small." He put his arm around Isabella and pulled her in for an affectionate kiss on the cheek. "A few more tweaks here and there and it'll be perfect."

"I don't think we ever get perfection. But for a small number of children, they get an alternative therapy. The more medical clinics and government agencies we can be affiliated with and be added to the referral list, the more people we can help," Isabella stated.

"I agree."

"Well, I hope we were able to help with your decision." Isabella looked at him and then at Belinda again as if she and Jesse were a couple.

"The decision has already been made. It's only a matter of how and who will get it done," Belinda replied.

Jesse didn't know how to answer, but suffered another playful punch to the arm from Dimitri.

They chatted a bit more about the business as they headed back to Belinda's SUV. A business that appeared so simple on the outside was far from that on the inside. Given the responsibility to the clients and animals, along with training and finding the right coaches, this was a major undertaking. Only someone who passionately believed in their mission could do this. Belinda, who stood next to him, hadn't disclosed an ounce of doubt as Isabella and Dimitri provided the good and not-so-good details. Those narrow shoulders impressed the hell out of him.

By the time they returned to the car, Jesse knew that he had had a change of heart, not that he had ever been against the project. But his awareness had broadened, and in his mental picture, he could see Belinda with her clients and full-service operation staffed with great trainers. While it had simply been a job for him to come in and work on, now he had a genuine desire to see it to fruition.

They waved goodbye to their hosts and headed back to the SUV.

Jesse waited until they had cleared the bumpy trail for the paved country road. "Miss Toussaint…"

"It's Belinda." She tilted her head, but didn't look at him, keeping her eyes on the road.

"No, what I have to say should be formal. Besides, it might be important for me to get it off my chest as I once again put my life in your hands on these windy country roads."

Only a small smile was her response.

"Miss Toussaint, I not only want to apologize for my rudeness and attitude yesterday. What you're doing is important and I want to be part of your team. I also want to request that you reconsider removing me from the project and reconsider taking the contract from my father. So, can I get a second chance?"

Belinda almost slammed on the brakes. Yes, things had thawed between them, especially after the tour of the facility. But she was playing in her head the various versions of her apology that would get him to come back. And now he wanted her to think about his return. As if she wouldn't jump on it.

"Mr. Santiago, I accept your apology. I would like to rehire you for the job." She wanted to leave it there, but her conscience poked at her. "And I'm also sorry for overreacting. As my cousins remind me, not everyone is a horse person."

She took his outstretched hand and shook it, then immediately returned her hand on the steering wheel. After sitting next to him, walking near him, all day, she was aware of his every gesture, movement, action. To press her hand against his palm signaled the beginning of their relationship. *Down, girl.* Purely business.

"You asked why I wanted to build a rehab facility." She glanced at his profile. Unlike the last time, he didn't show any reaction. He kept his gaze on the road ahead with occasional glances through his window. She continued, "Seven years ago, Maritza, my friend, had such an active life before the terrible car accident. She fell asleep at the wheel. One day, she's talking about her plans for the summer before heading to law school. We were off to celebrate. The next day, she's being pried out of a mangled car. Her life changed, like so many others who suffer sudden life-altering challenges—some physical, some emotional and cognitive. I want to do whatever I can to raise awareness and to provide real, tangible help…"

Dreamweaver Riding Program was more than her job. From the beginning, this idea had been personal. Sleepless nights of agony, mostly emotional, twisted her in their knots. Some people were inspired by a parent's job or a teacher's motivation. In her case, regret, guilt and resignation propelled her to build a sanctuary for young children with disabilities. With the expansion, she could consider adding adult clients, like veterans. That would be such a bonus benefit.

While her dreams were on the verge of turning into reality, she desperately wished that she could thank the person who inspired her. She kept the last photo that she'd taken of Maritza in a frame on her desk, as a reminder. She'd do anything to see Maritza smile like she did over their meal at Cracker Barrel in that photo. One selfish act, giving up the driving duty, and everything had changed because she'd caused Maritza to live the remainder of her life in a wheelchair.

"I get it. This is for her—a tribute."

Belinda nodded. "She inspired me. In one way, I wish that she'd never been in an accident. In another, I can't be certain that I would have worked this hard to put a facility in place, much less on my property, otherwise."

"Nevertheless, she must be proud."

Belinda didn't reply immediately. She couldn't confirm that opinion. After the way that she and Maritza had dealt with the accident, their friendship had suffered the toll. All she had were the memories and photos. Now her best friend no longer spoke to her. She held on to a sliver of hope that they would reconcile. They were once travel buddies. They knew each other's secrets. They had even planned to have a double wedding, even though neither one was dating at the time. Outside of her cousins, Maritza was her best friend.

Belinda sighed. "I hope that one day I do get to find

out how she does feel." But that was too personal a subject to share. "Well, we're here." She pulled up in the restaurant's parking lot next to his car.

"Okay." He placed his hand on the handle, but hesitated.

"What?" She waited, hoping it wasn't another apology. It wasn't the apology that had had an effect. It was the deep, velvety voice. He had a knack of adding a certain flavor to his words like a drop of the right spice in a meal that caused a warm flush. From there, her imagination and her body's tantalizing reaction to him dared to go to her uncharted fantasies.

He leaned in toward her. And she immediately responded by leaning toward him. Their lips touched, igniting a spark, bright and robust, enough to explode through her body. A kiss that didn't stop at the gate, but boldly marched to the front door. And with the thrust of his tongue intimately greeting her mouth, she opened the door to let him in.

A low moan escaped. She didn't care. The more he kissed, the more she wanted. His hands cupped her face. Her hands grabbed his shirt, fisting it as her desire surged. Warmed by her sensual cravings, every part of her submitted to his onslaught. Her nipples perked into hard beads. Between her legs, her panties moistened for action.

Jesse's mouth eased away without her permission. But he wasn't so cruel as to abandon her completely. His tongue snaked a trail along her jaw to her earlobe. On the tip, his lips gently kissed. And she threw her head back. A hot streak of hunger hit her hard. She wanted his mouth on her body, offering its own slavish devotion.

"Stop." Her hands were still entangled in his clothes. A moan of frustration bubbled up. Hers. She pulled away. Hot and bothered. "Um…damn, you are going to be so bad for me."

"I hope so," Jesse whispered. "But one thing I do know."

"What?" If she stepped out of the car at this very minute, she'd be on the ground. While her brain tried to regain balance, her body still reverberated over the kiss that he had laid down.

"I'm still hungry."

"I am, too." Her stomach rumbled on cue. "You don't have to get home?"

"Nah."

"Good." She failed at keeping her tone from sounding thrilled. "Mind grabbing a table while I park?"

"No problem." He stepped out of the car. The view of his rear at eye level drew an appreciative throat clearing from her. She stayed glued to her target until he disappeared into the restaurant.

Provide an apology.

Get recommitted to her vision.

Those had been her goals for today. But that searing, hot, nipple-hardening kiss. She sighed. Besides, she entertained a secret wish for part *deux* of their heated foreplay.

No doubts lingered. She wanted it all—Jesse Santiago naked and uninhibited between her legs.

Chapter 6

Belinda lay on her couch with the remote on her abdomen and an untouched bowl of caramel popcorn on the floor within hands' reach. Her cousins, Fiona and Dana, would howl with laughter to see her stretched out, looking at the TV station on home interior decorating. One, she wasn't the type to sit still long enough to watch anything on television. Two, she certainly wasn't the type to care about the comparative advantages of paint versus wallpaper. That's why Dana had taken on the task of decorating her new house after she moved in. The quaint country look, she'd remarked, didn't suit Belinda's tastes. Frills, classic soft blue and white colors, handcrafted knickknacks—not her style, but Belinda would have learned to live with the cozy, down-home feel out of sheer lack of motivation to do otherwise.

Like an angel on a charity mission, Dana had swooped in, armed with decorators and designers. Over three months, they performed surgery and transformed the house into an airy, modern home with a blast of natural lighting, vivid colors that Belinda would have never thought could be partnered, and furniture that still had comfort, but had more sleek sophistication. All in all, the do-over had been a massive success. Maybe a small part of Dana's desire to change the world, one fashion trend at a time, had a trickle-down effect to her. Hence her almost comatose position on the couch, watching home decorating tips and actually looking forward to the next show on how to build a flower box off a window or deck.

Her phone rang. She groaned and answered without her usual check to see who called.

"Belinda, it's Jesse. Letting you know that I'm on the property."

"Oh." Her body tensed like she was attempting a stomach crunch, sending the remote sliding off to the side.

"Won't be here long. I will let you know when I'm done."

Over the past two weeks, she'd done her best to avoid Jesse. Of course, once the work started, she had to give him direction and be available to answer questions. Anything else that threatened any form of intimacy, she did her best to run from. This wasn't the time to prove that she wasn't a coward. All she needed with Jesse was the perfect timing, skirting the pesky work details, and she'd be all over him, grinding against his body, seeking further satisfaction. With a voice like warm melted chocolate, her willpower would be no good. And she wasn't a chocolate lover. She hired the man do a job, almost fired him for not being up to par, and now had to fight against her temptation to go flirt with him on the job—a losing battle.

"Thanks." She disconnected the call. A triple shot of espresso with its mad rush to the system was the only comparison to how she felt at this minute. Under the influence of a hyper buzz, as she was now, lying back on the couch watching TV shows didn't satisfy.

Home decorating tips could take a hike. Something, or rather someone, way more interesting had popped onto her radar. Playtime was about to begin. She couldn't stop grinning, as her imagination ran free and a bit on the wild side. None of her cousins were here to talk good sense into her against her impulsive desire to go play. She tapped the phone against her chin, thinking about what to do next.

Belinda did her best not to hop up from the couch and speedwalk straight to the barn. The man had come to work. On her project, for goodness' sake. The least that she could do was actually let him do his job without acting like a flirty college girl in his face. To slow down her plan to charge into his domain, she headed for the shower.

Vanity had nothing to do with it. But instead of the standard shower gel, she reached for the moisturizing, coconut-scented body wash that promised all kinds of good things, like smooth skin that glowed. Music played in the background as the soundtrack for a thorough washdown. She soaped up *and* sang.

After drying off and adding a touch of her favorite scent on her neck and behind her ears, Belinda stood in front of her closet with an important decision to make. Standing around at the stable was not supposed to be the epitome of a fashion moment. Likewise, she didn't want to look like a rough-and-tumble field hand. She sighed. It wasn't fair that the law of attraction only had one player in the equation. Because, darn it, she noticed him. Bottom line, she wanted to be noticed. Ever since he kissed her, he hadn't tried again. Instead, Jesse became the consummate professional with everything from his management of the workers to his formal updates on the project and his responses to her questions with an exact, stay-within-the-lines demeanor. In return, her self-exile was to keep herself from grabbing his face and kissing him until the sun went down.

What she wanted out there—Jesse's attention—and what was available in her closet didn't work together. Frankly, the breadth of her clothing options was pitiful. Not her words. That would be Dana and Fiona not hiding their opinion about her distant position on the ladder of steps to being considered a fashion icon.

All her life, her style had been pretty much unchanged. She was a jeans and plaid shirt kind of girl. When it came to dressing up, she opted for pantsuits with solid-color silk tops. Shoes were her weakness, though. On the right occasion, she was known to rock a four-inch heel with a pair of well-worn jeans.

Today—more specifically, this minute—she wanted sexy casual. Not her usual ragtag, untidy and disheveled casual. No, this should be more a *controlled* kind of casual that could make Jesse look twice.

Impressing wasn't the goal. The man worked for her. He needed to impress her. However, there was that bit of reality, in which her attraction to him expanded the longer she was in his company and was bleeding over into the quiet moments when he wasn't around. In those times, she relied on memories of him in his T-shirt that showed off his bared sinewy arms. Despite the dark-colored T-shirts that he chose to wear, the outlines of his ripped body weren't difficult to discern. Muscles along his back stretched and contracted as he worked, and she spied. Occasionally, he'd bend to pick up a plank of wood and she'd need to take a deep breath. His behind was firm and tight and outlined by relaxed, fitted jeans. If he looked this sumptuous with clothes on, he had to be rocking it without a stitch. And when those thoughts entered her mind, she'd retreat from her hiding spot to head back to her side of the fence.

Belinda dressed, opting for black jeans and a black T-shirt. So much for spicing things up. But she didn't want to look pressed for his attention. She didn't have a public notice of a man vacancy that needed to be filled. And she wouldn't be trolling her workplace for such candidates, no matter how handsome they were. This was strictly a window-shopping, eye-candy event that her cousins would endorse, maybe even participate in, if they were here.

Except for Dana. Her romance with Kent had been a battle of the wills with a beautiful ending. She sighed. One day she wanted to fall just as hard for the right man. Nothing kept her from thinking that it wouldn't happen. But with her business and most of her time spent on the property, she didn't stand much chance of meeting someone.

"Heck, the man would have to come rolling into

my life like tumbleweed and knock me off my feet," she remarked to her reflection in the mirror.

The man—Jesse. Rolled in—as substitute contractor. Blew her off said feet—every damn day and night. Waking up sexually hot and frustrated, only to finish off the job with some self-loving, wasn't how she wanted to segue from dreams to reality. She wanted complete satisfaction from the real deal and not from batteries and a vibrator. All she had to do was picture Jesse standing stark naked, only in his construction boots, and her body sprung into meltdown mode.

Belinda fluffed out her hair and gave it free rein to fall on her shoulders. Not wanting to look staged or pressed for his attention, she opted for no makeup. The black legging jeans hugged her body in all the right places, especially with her T-shirt tucked in. She stood in profile and nodded in approval at what she saw. The right bra pushed up her boobs. All outward assets were on display. She smiled. Time to go play.

She headed from her house with two cold bottles of beer. Trying to pretend that she didn't want to see him was stupid. She was a grown woman. A horny grown woman.

If things had the right flow, she'd talk to Jesse about the job, discover what his plans were along the way and find out if there were any unforeseen issues about the riding ring that she needed to know, sooner than later. That would take care of the business side of things. Then she could take a spin on the personal side.

Her walk took her past the office. She had to fight the urge to go in and work. Mounds of paperwork sat on her desk awaiting her attention. Grants had to be written. Supporters of her cause had to be contacted to transition them from interested individuals to donors. After several long days of nonstop activity, her body was in a state of rebellion with constant headaches, muscle pain and trouble focusing.

It took Tawny jumping on her soapbox and laying down the bit of common sense that if she wasn't functioning at one hundred percent, the dream that she wished to fulfill could be compromised. Taking her friend's advice, she had shut off her computer and promised to rest over the weekend. Prowling after Jesse might not be considered R & R.

As she got closer to the stable, the sound of hammering grew louder. Since she didn't see Jesse in the riding ring, she figured he was in the stable working. With the particularly warm day, she didn't blame him for seeking the shade, even though the humidity was pushing her limits to stay outdoors. The last thing that she wanted to resemble was a soggy black crayon. Maybe she should have gone for a brighter color.

Music with a mixture of Latin and hip-hop beats played from an unknown source. It was not blasting, but played at a comfortable volume to accompany his industrious undertaking. It took a good minute for her eyes to adjust to the dark interior before she proceeded ahead. She also didn't want to surprise him while he handled any dangerous equipment.

The hammering stopped and the nail gun went to work along two planks of wood. Good to see that he could work just as hard without her hovering, a point he made sure of telling her after he kept running into her. However, part of her hovering had a serious edge.

She wasn't one to rely on words and good intentions. Not when it involved her project.

Action spoke volumes. Her heart picked up its hard beat in reaction to the fluid movement of Jesse at work. How could she behave without the slight shiver of excitement? More than her heart reacted. Her body stood at attention, nipples budded to hard peaks, hot desire awakening deep in her belly, the hidden juncture between her legs moistening with its sensual dew.

Jesse worked with his back toward her. One additional detail caused a hitch in her breathing. He worked in only his pants. Although he stood partly in the shadows, enough light from the window on the upper deck of the barn filtered down in a dusty arc to show off his physique.

Not a sound. Not an exhalation. She did nothing to give away her presence…yet. Admirers in a museum had the time to ponder, analyze and soak in notable statues. What her attention fastened on—his body—certainly could be mounted on a pedestal. It was bold, unique and powerful with the sheen of sweat that enhanced the curves and cut of his muscles.

Watching the perfectly created male model, she wanted to drink in the maple-brown hue of his skin tone. That suffused light added a majestic touch to his physique during the moments when he didn't move. As he surveyed his work, his body remained still, his profile strong and manly; a quiet stately aura of strength and power settled on him.

Belinda placed one of the cold beer bottles against her cheek and then her forehead. This hot flash had nothing to do with weather conditions. Every inch of him could have been sculpted as the epitome of male beauty. Wide, toned shoulders anchored the body with a tapered line to his waist and hips. Her gaze slid down, slow and appreciative, to settle at his waist.

Not only did her gaze land on the lower half of his body, it lingered. Faded, worn jeans hung with a sexy drape on his hips. The edge of the waistband showed off the brand of his underwear. Not a designer tag. The revelation worked for her. He was a man who chose simple and solid for his basic needs.

Her mind had wandered to a what-if scenario. What if, under different circumstances, they found each other attractive? What if they acted on the impulse to hang out, catch a movie or visit a bar?

The beer bottles clinked together. Her hands had moved involuntarily, broadcasting her presence.

He spun around, hammer in hand like a weapon... like Thor's hammer, only human-size.

"Hi, Jesse." Belinda held up the beers.

He took the beer without hesitation, and saluted her before taking a long swallow.

On the outside, she bore down on herself to remain cool and unaffected. On the inside, her nervous system remained at a heady spike that ran rampant without an emergency exit for the much-needed release.

He grinned. "I'm impressed. You knew exactly what I needed."

Where was this man's shirt? She tried not to fan her face. *Play it cool.* The only way she could manage any kind of conversation would be to avert her eyes. Impossible. She did try to not look at him. Off to the side of his face, there was a tiny scar between his eyelid and brow. Right there, she pinned her focus. Otherwise, looking into those deep, distant eyes was

a bit like staring into the sun—a blinding, enthralling moment that didn't release any secrets.

Now closer, she not only saw the flawless beauty of
his skin, but also the matching physique of his front.
If only she could touch, trace with her fingertips, the
sleek athleticism born for the arduous job of running
up and down a soccer field.

"Did you need something?" he prompted.

*I want you to stop asking me questions that you re-
ally don't want the answers to.* Well, that's what she'd
like to say. Instead, she replied, "Taking a break...
from taking a break. I'm supposed to relax and give
the brain a rest this weekend." She rolled her eyes.
"Per Tawny's persuasion."

"I've only been here two weeks, but from where
I stand, I'd say you do deserve a break." He grabbed
his T-shirt, which was hanging on the edge of a plank
of wood.

Good, cover up that hot temptation before she sank
into a puddle of drool. But damn, she didn't want the
live feature to end.

"Oh, please, you don't have to put it on for my ac-
count." She waved away any notion of prudish sensi-
bilities. She'd much rather watch the washboard abs
do their dance to accompany his movements.

"It got hot," he explained in an apologetic tone.
In one smooth movement, the T-shirt slid in place,
covering up what she instantly missed after the short
time span.

"How are things in general?" She tried to refocus
and worked to pull in general safe topics.

"Pretty good. Things are pretty much going as
planned. I may need to bring in a few hands to do

the heavy job of adding more fencing. You said that you wanted to open the ring."

Belinda nodded. "I want various rings. I want several clients at a time to be able to ride in their respective areas."

"Cool. You know, I have to say that it really helped going to Sunny Dale to see their setup. I'd heard of horse-riding therapy. Had no idea how much work it took to run the place. To see those kids and the trainers, the horses…it was such a team effort. I was blown away by it all." He wiped his hands on a towel. His gaze was downcast; his voice dropped to just above a whisper. "Sunny Dale has two people at the top in its operations. I hate to state the obvious, but there is one of you."

"Yeah, I hear that constantly. I think about it even more." Belinda hoisted herself onto a bundled set of wooden planks. "All it means is that I have to start smaller, slower. I have to be smart about everything. Nothing new when it comes to running a business, right? You'll see when you take over from Ed."

"My dad will be head of Santiago and Sons Construction for a long time. No complaints here. Still have to figure out what I'm doing. Right now, I'm only following orders." He looked down at his hands where a few Band-Aids covered several cuts.

"Please. You are the expert negotiator when you want things your way. Don't think I don't know when you're twisting my arm," Belinda teased.

"I'm simply getting you to think of different approaches."

She grunted in agreement.

"You can't deny that adding an indoor ring wouldn't be a bad idea?"

"I wouldn't argue to a lot of your suggestions, except those adjustments add thousands of dollars to my bottom line."

"But in the long run, you'll enjoy my wise counsel." He chuckled when she blew a raspberry.

"I've doubted myself over this project for a while now and probably will continue to do so, to some extent. But I feel, in my heart, this is the right thing for me to do."

"Good for you. You've got spunk. I like a woman that will take charge and conquer a hill or two." He raised his bottle and she tapped the neck of hers with his. They synchronized their long swigs in her honor.

With such a rousing compliment, Belinda felt as if she could stay perched on her hard resting place and watch this man for the entire length of the afternoon. Her face still held its blush. Looking at him continue to drink and talk about what he was working on, she wanted to figure out this man. Figure out the real reason for his break from soccer. Figure out what brought him home. Even if he'd left of his own accord, he didn't have to come here. She couldn't imagine that he didn't leave a heartbreak or two in his wake. Belinda wanted to believe that his single status was legit.

She asked, "Why did you come to work today? On a weekend?"

He walked to the doorway and looked out. "It's quiet here. You're not close to the main roads. There isn't the mad crush of people." He slowly turned to face her. "The view is breathtaking." A sexy smile turned into that familiar cocky grin.

Attraction…from him? Dare she hope?

"Plus, I'm not doing anything at home. So, why not?" He shrugged and approached, stopping inches before her. "And I'm not sure if I've made it to your good side, as yet."

"I thought we had ironed out the ripples. And therefore, we're good." Belinda had never thought that he could think she was offended or still held some misgivings. The man was too quiet for his own good.

"The kiss…?" He wound the towel in his hand. Worry creased his brow.

"I'd say it was a 9.25."

"Huh!"

She explained in a lighthearted tone, "Technique was good—"

"Good?" He shook his head. "You were moaning as soon as our lips touched. That's more than good."

"Fine. Excellent. Delivery, exceptional. Follow-through…didn't really maximize."

"Not my fault. You were the hungry one who had to go in the restaurant."

"And no follow-up. No information on what to do for a repeat performance." Belinda licked her lips. Even though she teased, she did expect him to play to his bad-boy image. Instead, he was the perfect gentleman.

"Well…I'll take that under advisement." He paused as if considering the situation. "I didn't want to have to hope that you wouldn't kick me off the job."

She shook her head. Obviously, their tentative approaches dampened the impulse to go after what they both had felt. Well, she didn't need a do-over. Simply a continuation would suffice.

"You said that there wasn't anyone waiting. Kind of hard to believe. You know that you're a triple threat."

"Triple?"

"Good looks. Multitalented. Successful." Belinda counted off on her fingers.

"What does that mean?"

"Marriage material. On some woman's internet board, you're pinned to it under fantasies that may come true."

Jesse laughed hard. After several seconds, he shook his head. "Trust me. I'm free and clear."

She melted.

"Playing soccer didn't afford the time for dating. I'm not claiming to be an angel. But I'm a careful person when it comes to entanglements. And I check character references."

"How many references do you normally need?"

"Two. If I need more, then something isn't quite right, don't you think?"

She shrugged. "I've never done character references. But my dating schedule has been pretty empty."

"And did you come to regret those dating experiences?"

She thought about her most recent past relationship. A character reference would have saved her much agony. "What if you already know the person? You see them every day."

"Like a friend?"

"Not sure if that's the status. But hopefully it's much closer to friend than to enemy."

"Then a reference is optional. A simple test could help determine the go-ahead status." He took hold of both wrists. "May I?"

"What are you doing?"

"I'm skipping the reference part."

"But you only ask for references if you are interested in the person." Belinda looked down at Jesse's hands circled around her wrists.

"That's right." He paused. "I'm interested. Very interested." His announcement was barely above a whisper, an intimate declaration that left him and zeroed in straight on her heart.

"So am I," she gushed with a shy smile. "Interested. Very."

"You answered truthfully." He released her wrists.

She stroked the small area that had been covered by his hands. If he only knew that he'd opened a door that she might not be able to close.

"I'm going to get back to work." He lightly flipped her hair away from her face. "And you're going to head back and relax."

She licked her lips. Everything was dry.

"And then I'll get cleaned up and pick you up to head out to dinner."

"Okay. But allow me to show off my culinary skills. Why don't you come over for dinner?" She waited. The train had left the station and she had taken a seat in first class to enjoy the ride with all the perks.

"May I?" He took the last step before standing in her spot.

"May you...what?" She desperately needed that drink.

"Kiss you."

She nodded. "Kiss me."

Before he could make the first move, she took hold

of his head. Gentle, even if excited, she pulled him toward her and kissed him. A simple act of pressing mouth against mouth. The chaste kiss had enough impact to rock her to the core.

"Lady, for once, let me lead." He spoke softly against her mouth.

"My bad. All yours."

"Hush." This time, his hands were the guides, holding her head still. His body fit between her legs. Her chin raised under the power of his finger. "Close your eyes."

She complied as the gap between their faces gradually closed.

Gentle. With a soft touch, featherlight, his lips brushed hers. Yet its connection pulsated with megawatt power. His mouth slid over hers, pressing its warmth and request to enter. Belinda had no reservations about offering an open welcome. She gripped his T-shirt, holding him in place, although they were already locked in each other's grasp.

Their mouths danced a slow waltz in tune with their own beat. His arms embraced, drawing her into his chest. He led. She followed. Their rhythms combined in a heated parry of tongues. She pressed her breasts harder against the brick wall of his chest. Definitely not the only place that hungered for him. Her thighs pressed against his, wanting more, needing and hungering for *all* of him.

She broke free. Her lips practically pulsed like a sound wave after the effect. Her chest rose and fell. "Damn, you're good. A 10." She nodded. "Definitely, a 10."

"And I'm still willing to make a fantasy or two come true…for you." He winked.

"Hurry and finish up here," Belinda begged. "See you at the house."

"Can't wait." Jesse sent her off with his sexy grin.

Back at the house, Belinda couldn't sit still on the couch. Her mouth still tingled in happy recall of each kiss. The man had a stronghold on her emotions. But she wasn't worried that the one-way road still existed.

The bulge in his pants had spoken volumes. No words necessary. She'd wanted his *attraction*. From her vantage point, he had more than a little attraction. And that was just fine with her.

Her fingers trailed the outline of her mouth, running over the surface that he'd kissed. She pressed them against her lips, hoping to replay the pressure of his mouth. Only the real deal could make her panties wet with desire that she could barely contain.

Now she acted like a college girl prepping for a date. Restless and excited. Her nerves hummed on a frequency level that only needed Jesse's response. Thank goodness no one needed to see her pacing in at the window, where she had a constant lookout. No sign of Jesse yet. Besides, he had to leave to clean up. How to stay occupied until he arrived?

Her phone buzzed. She looked down at the text from Fiona.

Feel like a movie later?

Belinda typed, Can't.

K. Staying in?

Nah. Got a date. Belinda couldn't deny the ego-driven smugness with that nugget. Her cousin would definitely not let that bit of news pass without comment.

Sure enough, her phone rang. "Hello, Fiona. What can I do for you?" She couldn't stop laughing.

"Don't play with me. Spill. I want every word. No shortcuts."

"Remember I told you about Jesse, the contractor who I fired?"

"Nooooo." Now it was her cousin's turn to laugh heartily. "Figured there was something else floating around over the entire affair."

"It's not that funny." Belinda defended, not sure if the joke was on her. "It was a mutual thing. Grown-up-like."

"Yeah, you hussy. You've had your eyes on him ever since he walked into your office."

"But I didn't act on it until I knew for sure that he also felt the same way. I don't plan to be the type of woman pining over a man." That was for dreams at night.

"Good to hear. Don't want to lose you over some dude. Remember Lionel Waters? Handsome, but a big jerk. Now you know that Dana and I have to meet the man in charge of snagging my big cousin's heart."

"Snagging my attention? I have my heart on lock-down. And don't mention Lionel. It took too much effort to get him to finally take no as no."

"I'll back off…for now. Where are you going on your date?"

"We're staying in. I offered to cook."

"See, you are a romantic."

Belinda jumped in. "Not listening."

"Whatever. Dinner is more private. You can sit and hang out as long as you like. And you already know that you can cook like a master chef. Look at you putting a spell on your man." Fiona's teasing got Belinda to laugh, dispelling some of her nerves.

She didn't brag about her cooking to many. A short stint at culinary school provided enough knowledge for her to play in the kitchen with her own recipes. Between Fiona and Dana, they had mastered the art of begging her to cook them a Belinda original.

"Plus, by having it in your house, you have more control if you wanted to take him to bed."

"Fiona!"

"What? Don't you crave sex sometimes? I know you're not getting any. Heck, I'm not getting any. Need to take care of that." Fiona's voice drifted.

"I don't want to know your sex schedule. Let's get back to me."

"Does your dude feel like he has long-term potential?"

"Not so fast. We pressed lips together and that was about it. Nothing that says my bed is the next base for him to tag."

"I'm all for taking it slow and being careful. I'm a cop. But you are the most sensible person I know. Remember our message to Dana. The same applies to you. Go with the flow. So change your sheets with fresh ones, and spray some lavender over the linens."

"I'm beginning to change my perception of you." Belinda wrapped up the call with Fiona. She returned to the window to check for an update. The phone call may have distracted her long enough to have missed his departure.

And then there was her advice about the bed linens. Belinda headed to the hallway and pulled open the closet. Not that she had tons of bedsheet sets, but picking the perfect one wasn't a simple task. Flowers. Prints. Solid. Pastels. Would it even matter when they were locked in each other's embrace?

Belinda grabbed the nearest set and headed to her room. For good measure she lightly sprayed the air and let the scented water fall onto the sheets. Nothing might happen. Or a whole lot could go down. Either way, preparation and readiness were key to maintaining control of the situation.

Chapter 7

Standing at the front door, having pressed the doorbell, Jesse truly felt like a young man on his first date ever. Once more, he inspected the flowers he'd bought for her. The process of picking out each flower had taken longer than expected. They couldn't be bruised or wilted. Jesse wanted his bouquet to be a picture of perfection.

"Come in." Belinda opened the door. Her welcoming smile had the power to lift the nervous tension off his shoulders.

"You look beautiful." And she did. Her hair was loose and down on her shoulders, framing her face with only a hint of color on her lips. The sundress with its spaghetti straps hung loose, but still sexily draped over her body. Her creamy brown skin sparkled against the orange-red splash of color. Her bright smile reached down and stroked him awake. He had to control the urge to drop a kiss on her…just because.

"Thank you. Come in."

"You know I'm flattered that you want to show off your cooking for me." He placed his hand over his chest. "Honored." He was touched that she felt comfortable with him.

"Just means that you'll have to impress me next time."

"I'll do my best." He had no idea how he could possibly top her culinary skills. But in the meantime, he presented the flowers. "For you."

"I love tulips." She hugged him and quickly released with a breathy laugh.

"Now, if I'd bought daisies, you would have said the same thing." He barely recovered from the quick press of her body against his. Trying to be a gentleman was going to be difficult this afternoon. Their mutual attraction fed off their energy with a massive appetite, getting stronger and bigger. Like the rising bubbles in a corked champagne bottle, at some point there would be an explosion. And he looked forward to it.

"I do love tulips. One second." She headed into the kitchen to tend to the flowers. Minutes later, she emerged with them beautifully arranged in a simple glass vase. Also pinned between her arm and body was a small book. She set down the vase, then retrieved the book.

"What's that?" he asked.

"A book on flowers. I might be working on a flower box for the deck." She walked to the sliding doors and pulled back the curtains.

Jesse flipped through the book and easily found the chapter on tulips. He quickly read their history, from their beginnings in Turkey to the seventeenth-century tulip mania in Holland and its now worldwide place as a favorite. What quickly caught his eye was the expression that it conveyed was perfect love. Immediately his neck grew hot.

Love, the emotion, was so far from any goal in his mind. And the word *perfect*, when it came to him, didn't fit well and felt like a distant spot out of reach, a satisfactory state that he didn't feel he'd earned. His family bonds, in particular his relationship with Diego, were too rocky and deserved his attention to fix them. He snapped the book shut and handed it back to her. Why did she have to show him that?

Instead, he focused on the deck and the places she pointed to for the flower boxes. Those mundane details he could handle. They were hard, tangible tasks that were easy to accomplish, had a start and end date, and then allowed for movement on to the next project.

"Are you a vegetarian?" she asked as she headed toward the kitchen.

"Only when the meal may be unappetizing."

"I've got a couple pieces of salmon marinating."

"Salmon sounds good. Need any help in the kitchen?"

"No. But you can come and keep me company. I can find out what makes you tick." Again, she made his heart drop with her wide smile.

"What do you want to know?" He leaned against the open doorway leading into the kitchen. Waiting. She might be a fussy cook who didn't like to have interlopers hovering around her. Plus, he liked seeing her relaxed, smiling, talking without the wary glances she seemed to have reserved for him.

"Did you get kicked out of soccer for drugs? Last thing that I saw online."

"Well, now, don't hold back." That bold question had been asked as soon as he announced his retirement. Reporters had descended on the clubhouse with scenarios that would force him out of the league. Answers he wouldn't provide or that weren't salacious enough got embellished, until one reason seemingly stuck. He had been discovered using steroids. He had grown frustrated defending his skills and athleticism.

"Should I have asked a more acceptable question? I wanted to clear the air of any questionable stuff."

"I appreciate your directness. But I'm not, nor have I ever been, a user of drugs or banned substances. Clean bill of health. I had a choice of retirement to make and I made it."

She paused with her hands under the running water, her gaze on the window over the sink. "Do you ever second-guess that choice? Or the reason for taking it? Seems to me, from a client's perspective, that the decision has taken you way off the path. You don't ever want to be part of the pro-soccer world again?"

Jesse entered the kitchen and sat on the other side of the counter. "I entertain doubts on a daily basis. Maybe not as strongly as before, but they do swoop in. I've gotten this far on gut instinct."

"Have you ever been wrong?"

"Sometimes. But most times, I've been right." He wanted to add, *Like now, with you.* But his confession felt too personal and intimate.

She pulled out a bottle of wine from the refrigerator and poured two glasses. "Here's to good things happening because of it."

"They already are happening." He tapped his glass with hers. "Good and unexpected."

"I like that phrase. Makes me think of you."

Jesse had never navigated his social life blindfolded. Most of it, he controlled according to his rules. In the case with Belinda, the rules not only didn't apply, but his brain ceased to function on too many tasks.

He'd tried to stay out of her way. Obviously she wasn't going to help him with his plight. Showing up at the stable smelling so damn good. He knew of no other woman who could rock a pair of jeans like her. He didn't have to rely on memory with her standing so close. His desire wanted out.

Though absolutely refreshing and candid, Belinda was the exception to the women who threw themselves at him. When he'd first met her at his unfortunate firing, he'd wanted her. When she'd taken them to Sunny Dale, and he listened to more of her vision, his respect for her grew. Today when she stepped into the barn and watched him, it took everything in him not to turn and acknowledge her presence.

Her entrance had created a shift in the air. Her scent reached him as if mailed on express delivery straight to his nose. Surreptitiously, he checked her out, knowing the possible consequences. Hammering the nails could have ended with a bloodshot finger every time he inhaled that blasted perfume. Its vapor trail seductively hovered under his nostrils.

Right at that moment, he knew that he couldn't let her leave without telling her how he felt. His stomach had churned with so many nervous jitters that his condition embarrassed him. With every ounce of ego, he tried to maintain a cool facade. She didn't need to know how aroused he became when the smallest movement from her, such as licking her lips and playing with the strap of her dress, or the way her dress draped itself on her backside as she moved around the kitchen, spoke to him like a second language.

Belinda wished she could blame her runaway tongue on the wine that she'd sipped while cooking salmon. That wasn't it. This man had captured more than her interest. What the internet didn't provide in personal information, she aimed to get from him. Talking about silly things while making their dinner was a waste of time. With Jesse, time felt in short supply. She didn't hold back with what she wanted to know.

In those stormy, gray eyes, she sensed that he was sitting still in Midway for a quick minute. Then when the time was right, he'd lift off, maybe circle over for nostalgia's sake, before leaving. His interviews corroborated her theory with no mention of anyone, outside his family, who could anchor him. Soccer was the "other" woman in his life. She didn't believe that the breakup was clean or permanent.

"That was delicious."

Belinda slapped his hand away when he tried to clear the dishes. "Don't mistake this for domesticity. When you cook for me, it'll be my turn to sit back and watch you."

"There will be a next time?"

"Damn straight."

"Damn straight, it is." His smile turned into a wide grin.

She loaded the dishwasher and cleared up the kitchen. She accepted his compliments of his appreciation.

"Why so thorough with your questions? I feel as if I confessed everything."

She snorted. "I'm so sure that you didn't. But I'll take what I can get…until I get more." She dried her hands and poured another glass of wine. "Let's get comfy."

They settled in the family room. She deliberately waited to see which seating option he'd take. Single armchair. The love seat. The sofa.

The sofa it was, and he sat near the middle. At least they were on the same page. She dropped into the seat beside him and curled her legs beside her.

"Do I get to ask you a ton of questions?"

"Yep." She turned to him and rested her arm on the back of the couch. "Fire away."

"Why are you turning me inside out?"

"Because I want to sleep with you."

He coughed.

She clapped his back. "Water?"

"No. I'm good. Just…um…well, now."

"I'm not saying that we'll sleep together. I don't know if that was a thought in your head." She couldn't help but admire his handsome features. "I have a strong interest in the pursuit of such a possibility."

"Since you're on a roll, I don't want you to stop. The difference between possibility and reality is a fine line. Hopefully, when you sift through the information and make your plus and minus columns, the interest will increase."

He had no idea that not only had the interest increased, but had an intensity that stirred her anticipation. As fine as the outer package was, the inner spirit mattered more. They could BS their way by putting on a good show for each other, but she wanted to cut through the crap and not waste time.

"Is this your MO?" he asked.

"Explain." She had to touch him, any part of him. Sitting this close and only being able to admire without sampling or indulging in hearty helpings frustrated her patience.

"Is this how you go after your...targets?"

"That sounds predatory." She looked at his hands, wide and strong. Those fingers pressed against her flesh, finger-walking to sensual destinations along her body. Warm rush of desire unfurled. She squirmed in place. "I don't go after anyone. Men have approached me. We go out on a few dates. But I'm not interested in being a side thought. Not that I'm looking for a commitment ring, either. But booty calls are played out. With the business about to turn a corner in September, I don't have time for foolish behavior. I'm using the direct-approach method."

He didn't respond, at first. "I'm not the type to go in for booty calls, either."

"Not anymore," she clarified. "You did rack up quite a list there. Could have held your own beauty pageant."

"All exaggerations. The rumors gave me superhuman powers. At the end of the day, I was a professional soccer player, between training and matches, with not much time for anything else." He turned and leaned with a playful grin. "Have I earned my security clearance?"

She nodded slowly. "You haven't asked me a ton of questions."

"Figured I'd do that when we get cozy." His teasing remark was almost as good his touch. Almost.

"How cozy?" She bit her lip, thinking about nipping his.

He leaned over and kissed her. "Cozier than this." His breath brushed her mouth and she reached for the firm gentleness of his lips.

"Damn straight." She placed a kiss on his mouth after each word.

"Same time next week." He pulled back.

"Uh…"

"I'll be busy during the week. But I'll be back on Saturday to work."

"What if I don't want to wait?"

"You'll wait… I want you to wait." He delivered a kiss that curled her toes and rolled back her eyes. His tongue stroked her mouth, delivering the conditions of his contract. Her body trembled. Anticipation scrambling her senses. Hunger for him making her nuts. His fingers pressed into the flesh of her back. She arched into him, going after full body contact to quell the seductive fire raging in her. His thumb slid the strap off her shoulder and she moaned. Loud. Unladylike. Tenderly, he dropped a kiss on her skin. And she was wet.

He pulled back and readjusted her shoulder strap.

"What was that?" she asked, breathless and still turned-on.

"Just letting you know that I like to share the driver's seat."

"Next time, I'll give you the darn keys."

She needed a long, cold shower, and the major lack of sex had her fuming for the remaining hours in the afternoon after Jesse left.

Belinda peeled off her clothes and headed for the shower stall. Her mood was on the gray side of the spectrum, not quite murderous, but certainly not grateful. Jesse Santiago had wound her up like a mechanical doll and let her go with the promise that he'd be back in seven days.

When the day had started, she wasn't looking to get laid. She wasn't a one-night stand type of girl. And she wasn't about hopping into bed on a first date. But she'd never met anyone like Jesse.

Now she was left to think and fantasize about him for seven long days. He'd better be suffering as badly as she was. She punched her pillow, turned off the TV and lay in the dark, trying to make her body de-escalate from the raging craving for Jesse to do more than deliver panty-moistening kisses.

Not since Lionel Waters had any man seen her bedroom. That was a sort of good, safe friendship that had gone diagonally off the rails of sanity. Still, Lionel couldn't take no for an answer. At least his tries to get her back, as he always started his monologues, had dwindled over the past several months. She'd love for him to move on. But he seemed stuck in a groove.

Nothing in her had any intention of placing herself in a relationship to be reminded how much better off she would be with him or that her life would be nothing without him, Lionel's oft-repeated argument. At the time that they'd met several years ago, she had been hurting over her best friend's condition and their broken friendship.

Her father's criminal acts always cast a long shadow, which fed into her feeling very low about life. The emotional aftermath of the car accident didn't help her outlook. No doubt Lionel did provide a lifeline for her to emerge and take a second chance at living with purpose. Their years together shifted what she thought was a balance between them to his emotional manipulation and attempts to stifle and control her.

Once a supportive friend-turned-lover, he grew more obsessed with fixing her. His advice took on an edge of insistent demands. However, slow suffocation of her identity wasn't acceptable as payment. Finally, she'd had enough when he criticized her ties to the family. Even her cousins didn't escape his judgment. Grace evoked his greatest irritation with his condemnation that she ruled the business and the family like a tyrant.

It didn't help that, at their first meeting, Grace didn't connect with Lionel. Her shrewd intuition had picked up on his darker side. Her grandmother's warnings had gone unheeded. In Lionel's estimation, the family and the business should have no place in Belinda's life. She'd tie herself in knots trying to keep any meet-ups a secret. When he found out that she had a meeting with Grace about working at Meadows, he'd hit the roof that she not only attended the meeting without him, but didn't ask his opinion. The ensuing argument turned on the faucet to her emotions and frustrations. He'd committed his biggest mistake. No matter how damaged they all were or what dramas occurred, the family stayed together. With his overbearing manner, he'd sucked what little joy he'd brought to their relationship.

Now that she'd moved on, almost a year later, it wasn't that she had a no-entry sign on her bedroom for the next man. The situation never occurred because her free time to socialize and connect to anyone was severely shortened. With Jesse in the mix, she certainly could dedicate a few hours to her own self-interests.

Finally, Belinda, with a dreamy smile, drifted to sleep.

Jesse arrived on the work site every day and did his best to avoid Belinda. Work came first. It had to. He couldn't let his libido set the tone or his reputation. In seven days, there would be a repeat performance and he couldn't promise that he could take the high road and walk away.

His phone buzzed. A short text from Belinda.

Hope all is well.

Everything's cool.

See you later?

His fingers paused over the keyboard. Is it about the job?

Not really.

Then, Saturday. He added a smiley face to soften the message.

She responded with a frown emoticon. He chuckled and set down the phone. Time to get his head back on the job.

A familiar black SUV pulled up in front of the barn. Jesse remained where he was. Having a disagreement with Diego on his turf was one thing, but he wasn't going to allow him to bring their issues on the site. He waited.

"Hey, got a minute?" Diego took up a position opposite him.

Jesse nodded. His shoulders tensed.

"I've been thinking a lot about what you said. About what I feel. And…"

"Look, I get where you were coming from. Maybe I did walk from the family. The glitz and glamour can go to the head. Ain't gonna lie."

"It looked like it was fun." Diego relaxed his stance and Jesse followed suit. "I was kinda jealous of my big brother. Didn't think you remembered me."

"Remembered you? Heck, everyone around me knew about you. I was proud of you. Still am. Yale-educated. Studied abroad in England. Author of some boring crap." They shared a laugh.

Diego's face grew solemn. "You didn't come home, though. I wanted you here when I was in the hospital."

"Your asthma attack? I told Pop to keep me informed. I would have booked a flight immediately."

Diego looked down at his feet. "It was more than asthma. I wondered why you didn't come." He looked up, keeping his gaze away from Jesse's scrutiny.

"What happened?" Jesse remembered his father calling him the day before the championship game. He'd barely peeled off his training gear when the call came. His father had reassured him that it wasn't serious. Just one of those episodes that would knock Diego down for a day or two. He had thanked his dad, told him to keep him updated and then he went off to shower and study the game strategies for the next day.

Diego's various respiratory illnesses, especially asthma, weakened him and it meant that their lives always had to accommodate a health crisis or threat of one. Planned family vacations had to be cancelled. Pets had to be given away. Living on alert was a way of life.

Soccer came along when Jesse's adolescent frustrations got the better of him. Their father used soccer as an incentive and punishment to keep him in line. It worked. Jesse could plunge in and stay submerged and avoid a lot of the family goings-on. At the time, he'd counted himself lucky. And he hugged that sense of freedom hard. But now, with a sense of dread, he was about to find out how steep the price had been.

"What happened?" Jesse repeated. He closed the gap between his brother and him and gently touched his arm. "Tell me everything."

"It doesn't matter, right?" The smile on Diego's face looked forced. "I came over to say that I think we should call a truce and become friends again."

Jesse pushed aside his brother's hand and pulled him into a bear hug. "Deal." His throat squeezed with emotion. He pulled back and cupped his brother's face in his hands. "I want to know what happened."

"I had a collapsed lung."

"What? Why didn't they tell me?"

Diego shrugged. "I think we both know the answer."

Jesse kicked at the dirt. Regret flooded through him. Though his father kept the information from him, he understood how difficult it was to pretend that everything was okay. He knew that feeling quite well. "I promise that I'll make it up to you, bro." Jesse pulled his brother into another tight embrace.

"You can start by letting me breathe."

Jesse immediately let go. They laughed over his open affection. The air between them had changed. A swift current had pushed aside the toxic mash-up of guilt and misunderstanding. Now there was a spark of what they once had as brothers.

"Thanks for giving me another chance, Diego."

His brother nodded. "Dinner later?"

"Sure thing."

Jesse watched Diego drive off the property. The revelation still resonated. But he was thankful for Diego's reaction. Otherwise, the truth would have remained buried, fostering deeper bad feelings. He turned to resume his work. Maybe the reason for his return home wasn't as random as he'd felt. Something had been broken in his life. The fibers that once bound him to his family had unraveled. For the first time since his decision to retire, his mind and heart were on the same plane.

"Jesse?"

He spun around to see Belinda approaching him. "How did you…? Why are you here? Sorry."

"I came in from the back to surprise you. I didn't want to interrupt. But I also didn't want to sneak off like I'd done something wrong."

"You heard everything," he accused.

She nodded.

He couldn't bear to look into her eyes, to see the

indictment there. "Well, go ahead. You think that I'm a horrible brother. Hell, I know it."

She reached out for him, but he ignored her touch. Holding her in his arms was a reward. The way he felt didn't deserve the warmth and soothing pleasures of her touch.

"I can't have a do-over."

"Unfortunately, we can't. But you don't have to do anything over. Your brother has opened the door for both of you to heal and move on. Don't squander it. That's the lesson to be learned."

He nodded.

"I envy you."

"Why?"

"Your family operates like a unit. A team. Yes, your father put you first, but really he was making the best decision for everyone. Like a father, he tried to please both sons in the way he knew how." This time she didn't wait for him to hold her. Instead, she hugged him, resting her head against his chest. Her hands clasped behind his back. He pressed his cheek against the top of her head in the silky softness of her hair. "My parents operate as a team, a two-person team. I'm the third wheel that's not quite attached, but is there. No drama. No fights. It's a relationship of logic and responsibility. For the warmth and family love, I've learned to rely on my cousins and even my scary grandmother." Her laugh rumbled against his chest. "I don't want to ever get to the point where I'm just living. Where life is reduced to cold calculations and plus and minus columns." She removed herself from his arms.

His body immediately craved the imprint of her body. He wanted much more.

"I want to feel alive." She stared up into his eyes.

"Me, too." He kissed her, thanking her for tossing him a lifeline.

Chapter 8

"I have wine. Lasagna. French toast with garlic butter." Jesse waited for Belinda to give in and accept his invitation. He'd raced home and cooked everything necessary for a perfect date night. In between stirring pots, he managed to perform light housekeeping. There was not much prettying up to do with the houseboat, but it did smell much better.

"And...?"

"Soft music. Candlelight, if you want. Dessert."

She cleared her throat. "I have that at home. And my pajamas."

"You won't need it. And I have a romantic movie."

"So far, not really feeling the need to jump in my car."

Jesse tried again. "Would a back massage get you there?"

"Keys in hand. What else?"

"A scalp massage."

"Hmm. Keep talking."

"The rest is a surprise." Jesse had a few ideas. Mostly he wanted to improvise the moment.

"Near the office door. You're making me leave early. Better be worth it."

"Have you as the dessert. Whipped cream. Cherry. Warm caramel sauce." Jesse paused for her response.

The chime of a car door opening was the only sound coming through the phone.

"Then I'm going to lick it off you. A little at a time."

"You need to give me your address."

Jesse gladly provided the information to the marina. Now that he knew she was on her way, he wanted to make sure everything was in place. "See you in fifteen minutes."

"Bye."

Jesse used every minute of the fifteen minutes that it would take Belinda to arrive to prepare. By the time she called him that she was on the dock, he was breathing heavily, but showered, dressed and ready. He popped up out of the boat and beckoned to her. After he helped her on board, he opened the door and, with a grand gesture and slight bow, invited Belinda in.

She walked past him, but it was more like a strut in a little black dress. The short style exposed the length of her legs, which were crowned with red shoes with skyscraper heels.

"All this for little ole me?"

"Are you complaining?"

"Not at all." He pressed his mouth closed and mimicked turning the lock.

"Wine, please?" She took a seat and crossed her legs.

Jesse almost popped.

"I'll help myself. You seem to be…overwhelmed. You don't mind, do you?"

"From casual to hellafied sexy, I like all your styles."

"That's good to know. I do have a few more… maybe they'll come out to play later on." She poured wine into two glasses and slid one toward him.

Jesse studied the glass. He didn't want wine. He didn't want lasagna. His gaze lifted to Belinda's mouth, watching her swallow the wine. Afterward, her lips remained moist. He softly brushed his thumb across her lips, wiping them dry.

The tip of her tongue swept the pad of his thumb.

He hissed out a breath.

Her mouth opened and sucked in his thumb. Her tongue swirled and caressed. The dark gaze pinned him with a bold invitation, a proposition he was only too happy to respond to by scooping her against his chest. He headed down the hallway to his room, nudging it open with a foot.

His legs were willing to give way under the heated kisses against his neck. Not before he laid her gently in the middle of his bed. The little black dress shielding her body made her look like a gift to be unwrapped.

"I hope you weren't too hungry." Jesse unbuttoned his shirt, peeled it off and tossed it to the nearby chair. It missed. He didn't care.

"Figured that I'd get full on something else." She

eased herself out of the dress. Every move, sensual and alluring, pulled him to join her. "I found that the bra and panties didn't add anything to the outfit." She lay back on the bed in a glorious state of nakedness. Her tiny smirk let him know that she wasn't going to play fair.

Jesse quickly unzipped his pants and was out of the clothing within a few seconds. Socks included.

His mini strip show drew her applause. His erection strained against his underwear. A greedy and happy performer. But he wanted to take it slow and enjoy everything about this moment. He admired it all from her heart-shaped face down to her breasts, topped with puckered nipples that looked like drops of chocolate. Her body was toned with the right amount of thickness to fill his hands. His admiration continued down her abs that pulled in, as if he'd touched them with more than his gaze, down to the triangular patch where he couldn't wait for his tongue to meet her acquaintance and bury itself in her cave to feast on her.

Once his eyes took their fill, he followed up with his hand to continue the exploration. Lightly, he traced the outlines of her muscles, along her neck, down over her shoulders and arms. He picked up her hand and sucked each finger. She squirmed under his examination. Her giggles were muffled in the pillow. Her feet flutter-kicked with the sudden change of his trail down the center of her to her breasts, along her abs, over her belly button to the tip of her mound. He branded her.

In a quick scoop, his hand slid under her, cupping her behind. He flipped her without effort. "I want to admire all sides and angles of you," he whispered in her ear. "Your ass is sexy as hell." He stroked the fleshy mound and curves of each globe. Smooth, brown and gloriously replete. He didn't want to let go. His groin hitched, begging for its own action. Not yet. Instead, he traced his tongue along the middle, down between her thighs.

Her butt hitched up in the air and eased back down.

"I feel like I'm going to faint," her voice squeezed out. She hitched her butt higher. Poised. "I'm so wet."

"Let me check." His fingers beat a rapid two-fingered rhythm against the sensitive flesh.

She moaned.

Slowly, his fingers brushed over her clit. She pushed back.

"Don't move," he ordered.

She reached for his hand.

"I said, don't move."

"I'm going to scream."

He lapped at her labia and clit. Bold strokes. Rough. Unrelenting. Sucking in and releasing her. Over and over. Now her behind bucked for more attention. Again, her hands got in the way.

"I'm going to tie you up," he threatened, hating to pause in his ministrations.

"And then?"

"I'm going to have dessert," he promised.

Belinda giggled. "I'll tie myself to this bed." She reached for a tie that was draped over the headboard.

Jesse plucked it from her hand and made fast work of the tie. She could pull at his makeshift restraint and it would be loose whenever she wanted. In the meantime, he headed to the kitchen, gathered what he wanted and returned.

"I don't like to be kept waiting."

Jesse smiled at her impatience.

"Are you listening to me?"

Jesse flipped open the lid of the caramel sauce. They were going to have a brownie sundae. It looked like he was going to be the one to enjoy a sweet, delicious brown treat. With a slight motion, he dropped a thin drizzle of caramel between the space of her belly button and curly mound. Sweeping lashes of his tongue wiped it clean. Her legs crossed and uncrossed. He enjoyed the view of her sex ready to be picked and enjoyed. Once more, he trailed a thin drizzle of caramel sauce between her legs and followed up with a healthy spray of whipped cream.

"Aaah." She gasped and writhed.

He nudged her legs apart and settled in. This was one meal he had no desire to rush. He took his time eating, bathing her from top to bottom, bottom to top. For extra measure, he swirled his tongue in her wet cave, loving the mix of her and the sundae dressing. This was his dessert, all his. And he was going in for seconds.

Once he was done and Belinda's moans had quieted, Jesse switched up with his method of conquest. Gathering a mouthful of ice chips, he settled in and slipped as many as he could into her. She jerked under him. Her moans grew guttural. She begged him to take her.

He discarded his underwear and donned a condom before untying her.

"Please don't make me wait." She wrapped a hand around his shaft and squeezed, rubbing his balls.

Jesse had restrained himself from the start. The minute her hand touched him, he almost lost it. She opened her legs and thrust up her hips. With her nod to him, he held on to her shoulders as he came in for the landing. But there would be no taxiing. As soon as he thrust, they lifted off.

Her legs closed around his hips. The strength in her clasp thrilled him. He pushed deeper inside her. They worked together. She took and he gave, hard, fast.

"More, dammit."

Jesse scooped his arms under her legs and pulled them up. Her uplifted hips took his downward plunge and held tight to each stroke before letting go. Her warm sheath drove his mind into a whirl as their frenzied dance escalated. For all he knew, he could be floating and it wouldn't matter.

They were heading to parts unknown together. Her fingers locked onto his back.

He lowered her legs. And she promptly pushed against him.

"Pull me up onto you."

He was too giddy to resist her demands.

"I want to ride you to the end."

"Well, sweetheart, you'd better grab on to something." Jesse scooted to the edge of the bed so that his feet could be on solid ground.

Belinda faced him. Her eyes were bright and focused on his face, peering into the depths of his soul. They were at the peak, hand in hand, readying to jump off together.

"Hold on tight." The ride began with him lightly

lifting her off his lap. Within seconds, they were soaring together. She slid up and down his shaft, grinding in for good measure. The pressure built, pushing and surging. The flood grew powerful. Nothing would hold it back. Not that he wanted it to.

"Come with me," she screamed. Her head tossed back. He felt the tremor of her walls pulsating against his shaft.

Together, they burst through the last remaining wall between them. Wrapped in each other's arms, they stayed the course as wave after wave of release shook through them. Their descent back to solid reality came with the best memories to hang on to.

Belinda looked up to see why Tawny hovered at her desk. Today, her hair had transformed into a vivid burgundy with a throwback '70s mushroom hairstyle. If she had bad news, Belinda wished that she'd spit it out.

"Oh, I don't want anything," Tawny remarked. Yet she didn't budge.

"What are you looking at?" Belinda followed her line of sight.

"It's the calendar." Her assistant pointed at her desk. "The *X*s?" Her frown settled in, as she waited for an explanation.

Belinda looked at the blue *X*s that she'd drawn through the week on her calendar. "It's a countdown."

"A countdown? To what?"

"Nothing work-related." Belinda closed the book to make her point.

Tawny backed away with her hands up. "You know you can't keep a secret." She spun around and headed to the door. "By the way, Dana wants to stop by with potential donors. She said, probably this afternoon or tomorrow morning, maybe even later."

"Why?" Her cousin was supposed to be handling the fund-raiser. "There's nothing to see at the site. And now I have to be ready for possibly two different times."

"The site is coming along. But Jesse has made good progress. The ring looks great. The stable renovation is coming together. Pretty soon you can have the Northeast Equine Therapy Association come in and review for their certification."

"Yeah, but I'd rather these people just write the check and stay off the premises. Don't need anyone poking around until it's up to par."

Tawny laughed. "You don't have to be here. I can show them around the place."

"Thanks, but Dana would kill me for not being here, and then kill you for taking my place."

They both laughed. Dana's temper did have a far-reaching reputation. The cousins found it easier to avoid the eruption of her Vesuvius-like tendencies. As they got older, those volatile days were long gone, but they liked ribbing each other over her behavior and the usual fallout that involved all of them.

"Is Jesse on-site?" Belinda kept typing on the laptop. Her attention casually drifted from the monitor up to Tawny and then back down.

"No. Hasn't been around for the week. His workers are here, though. Ed came in earlier, too. But I could tell he wasn't ready for prime time. One of the workers took him back home within the hour."

"Caroline will not be happy. She'd warned me that

he was coming with Jesse. I think Jesse managed to be too busy to bring him along most days."

"Looks like Ed tried to do it himself."

"How did he get here? Please tell me that he didn't drive." Belinda shook her head when Tawny responded with a nod. These Santiago men were a stubborn lot.

"You want me to get Jesse on the line?"

"Nah. Not urgent. I was going to get a rundown on things in case I get any detailed questions from the donors." That sounded much better than *I'm suffering from a sexual hangover and need a repeat to cool my jets.*

"Gerard, the foreman for the next phase, is in charge. He stopped in at the office this morning to introduce himself. Big guy. Thick beard. Denim shirt. Regular Paul Bunyan type."

"Sounds like I shouldn't be able to miss him. I'll keep an eye out when I head out."

"That's it for the news."

Belinda nodded. Once Tawny left her office, she looked at her desktop calendar. Knowing that Jesse wasn't coming to the site, she took her blue marker and placed another *X* through the day. Every week he stayed out of reach and on the weekends, they'd get together. Now that it was Thursday, she felt like a woman dying for a drop of water while walking through a desert.

Her irritation was twofold.

One—she wasn't looking for a relationship. She wanted something temporary, fun, something to remember thirty or forty years from now.

Two—she wanted more than a mind-blowing

weekend booty call. They'd both said that wasn't a destination they wanted on this trip. But that was what it felt like as the weeks passed. Contradiction at its fullest about what she wanted, or didn't want, from day one.

Trying to chat over wood being sawed and nailed together had limits. And Jesse didn't seem to budge from his all-work-and-no-play rule during the workweek. It was like setting a bowl of ice cream on a table in front of her, spoon on the side, but she wasn't allowed to take any. She wasn't allowed to lean over the treat and steal a sample. All she could do was stare and look forward to any available day that she would be able to dig in and enjoy.

While it was easy to want to strip Jesse of his clothes, she also wanted to ease through that private, impenetrable emotional side. Yes, he helped set the rules. Was he tortured over the situation? If he was, then what was he willing to do about it?

Like there was in hers, was there a countdown in his head? A date to look forward to that made the skin erupt with goosebumps. Not only the skin, but every nerve felt ready to pop at the thought of his company. Never had she suffered such sweet agony over any man. Belinda sighed. The truth—Jesse Santiago was special. Seeking reassurance wasn't comfortable. Clearly she had the hots for him. And from their nights together, it hadn't been a one-sided affair.

Her phone rang, bringing her back to work. The reminder that she ran a business. One that required her undivided attention. There was no time to dwell on Jesse.

Tawny appeared in her doorway. This time she

held up a vase of tulips. "Oh my goodness, look what came for you."

Belinda took the gift and looked for a note.

"No note. I checked." Tawny shrugged. "Secret admirer?"

"Stop letting that imagination of yours go wild." Belinda turned the vase around to check for the note. Nothing. But really, did she have any doubts as to who it could be?

Her calendar. A vase of beautiful, colorful tulips. Her raging need to be writhing from serious love-making with her brooding hero. If she had a photo of him, all arrows would point his way.

Belinda picked up her phone and texted: Thank you. They're gorgeous.

To ensure that she didn't spend the next half hour staring at her phone for his response, she dropped it in her pocketbook and went back to work. Her life still had to go on. Even if she had to pretend that the butterflies fluttering in her stomach were nothing. Her anticipation for him kept escalating on a steep incline. And at some point, what went up would come down. Hard and fast. She just hoped that she'd survive the impact.

Her phone pinged.

Chapter 9

At three o'clock the *next* afternoon, Belinda greeted Dana and her small entourage of deep pockets. They smelled of money, old money, and were excited to find the next charity for their philanthropic appetites. If all the pieces fell in place, there would be a sizeable donation to be added to the operations, besides the planned fund-raiser.

"Sorry to drop in all unexpected," Dana whispered in her ear when they hugged. "It's difficult herding rich folk."

"You're the last one to talk."

"That's why I hang around you. I can feel like a regular citizen."

Now, that remark earned Dana a pinch on her arm.

Her cousin squealed with pain, causing the group to look over at them with concern.

"Behave yourself. Act like a business owner," Dana playfully admonished.

"One who is begging for money. Not a problem."

Dana introduced her to three siblings who really had an aura of old money about them. Their mother was a movie actress from a Hollywood dynastic line of actors and directors. Their father was a Yale professor and author of books that would hurt her head if she bothered to read about the philosophical greats. Together they were an unlikely mixture of social classes and backgrounds.

The siblings—Milton, Ronald, Portia—made her wish she had dressed like a British noble on a country estate. As if she had such clothing options in her closet. Instead, they would have to make do with her standard T-shirt and jeans. Dana had upgraded to her suits. Today, it was a black pantsuit. Belinda pasted on a bright smile and smoothed back the unruly strands of hair that escaped the ponytail.

"We are very excited about what you have here," Milton, who looked to be the eldest, remarked.

"Yes. Dana contacted us and I'm glad she did." Portia's impassive face didn't match her upbeat message.

"I'm very happy that you took time to come and see the facilities. Although, as you will see, it's still a work in progress. One that should be completed soon."

The third sibling remained silent. He never looked at her when she spoke. His attention flitted on the outskirts of their circle. While the other two weren't exactly brimming over with giddiness, his reserve had a chilling introspection. What was he doing here if he'd rather be anywhere else?

"Let's get going. Belinda, would you take us on a tour?" Dana prompted. Her raised eyebrows added the message that she should snap out of staring at Ronald—the imposing one.

Belinda led them out of the office. She'd already arranged with Tawny to drive them to the stables. Since she was the only one of the group dressed for the dusty walk, she followed behind the golf cart at a brisk pace.

Some days, like today, she'd look out toward the riding ring and stables, trying to see it like a newcomer for the first time. In her mind's eye, the horses would be freely running and cavorting in the paddock, an oasis of wellness within the lush green setting. Right now, the stable's exterior still looked worn and bruised. The appearance didn't matter now. Once all the interior work was completed, the final phase would be an extensive facelift on the building.

Like Sunny Dale's Riding Club, the Dreamweaver buildings would be bright and welcoming. The colors would match the bright hues on her house. She hoped that this family could see the potential and beyond the messy work in progress.

"Are we ready?" Belinda was a tad out of breath by the time she joined them. "Thanks, Tawny." She sent her assistant a silent message that she could leave. The parking area was closer to the stable and the siblings wouldn't need to be driven to their cars.

"Let's go." Dana hadn't taken that catering smile off her face. Her cousin did know how to wheedle cash from the many philanthropists.

Belinda ushered them into the stable.

"Wow!" Milton stepped away and walked farther into the building.

Even Belinda was awed. By deliberately avoiding the place since she'd invaded Jesse's work area, she hadn't seen the progression. The daily reports on paper didn't reveal the visual impact of what had been done. The extension built onto the stable had a massive domed frame with arching steel beams in place. The indoor facility had an open space that was perfect for bad weather and extra training time in a quieter setting.

"This is quite impressive," Ronald spoke. His tone remained cool, but he seemed to take note of every detail. At one point, he walked away to inspect the support beams of an area.

Belinda was about to explain the floor plan of the stable when Portia breezed past her. She swallowed her remark and followed Portia's steady march to see what caught her interest.

"Oh, he's here," Belinda said under her breath. She watched Jesse rise from his squatting position. Despite the fact that he was wearing a hard hat, safety goggles and had an unshaved face, she knew every inch of his body.

"Is that the great Jesse?" Dana chuckled.

Belinda didn't have to nod. She knew that her face said it all. Though no one might notice her blush, her entire body was fast-tracking to a nuclear meltdown. Not only was she flushed, but her muscles twitched and shivered with his close proximity.

Clearly Portia's sudden advancement startled him. The woman who didn't hide her interest in Jesse chatted for a bit, shook his hand and then pointed to their group. All his movements were slow, including his seeming reluctance to acknowledge them. While Portia grinned and gestured madly with her hands, he remained still, and attentive to the woman.

More than slight annoyance prickled her nerves. A smidgen of jealousy tweaked at her confidence.

The distance of several feet across the room didn't hinder Belinda catching every detail of his expression. She frowned. Jesse's coolness toward her wasn't a figment of her imagination. She knew the range of his expressions—cool professionalism toward Portia and frosty displeasure for her.

The heady excitement that almost took over her body retreated with a quick pace. The idea that he truly had been avoiding her hit her square in the chest.

"You can stand there like a statue. I'm going to meet him." Dana left her. Milton also hurried along. Only Ronald remained. But with his undead vampiric attitude, she wouldn't have minded if he did go with the lot.

"No, he's…busy." Belinda reached out to stop her cousin.

Dana giggled and promptly speeded up. "Hi, Jesse. I'm Dana. Nice to meet you. Heard so much about you."

Jesse nodded. His grumpy response looked as if they had intruded on his space. The way he pitched his glare toward her, again, Belinda guessed that he blamed her for the invasion. Well, she could be equally irritated with his avoidance issues. Even if he brought her to her knees in the bedroom, out here, she was his boss.

"Jesse, since you are here, would you give the O'Hares a tour of the facility? I'll be here for questions about the project."

The way Jesse tossed down the towel that he'd used to wipe his hands spoke volumes. Whatever. He didn't have a choice. Now he could play tour guide.

"My, my, lots of tension with a capital *T* between you and Biceps over there." Dana bounced along behind the group with her.

Belinda didn't bother responding to Dana's teasing. Instead, her focus was on Portia with the svelte figure, who maneuvered herself next to Jesse.

"I hope you're not letting the socialite get to you. But she is attractive, if you're into the perfect-doll look."

"Shut up." Belinda couldn't compete with perfection. In his former world, Jesse must have had his pick of the perfect females who fawned over him. She shoved her hands, which were badly in need of a manicure, into her pockets.

"You know, I didn't realize that soccer players had such fantastic bodies."

"What do you care? You have the British hunk all wrapped up and neatly whipped."

"Yeah, I do. Don't I?" Dana cocked her head and sized up Jesse. "If you play your cards right, you can nab him, too."

"He doesn't want to be nabbed." She didn't mean to sound disappointed. "And neither do I."

"Yeah, right." Dana gave her a one-arm hug and rubbed her arm. "Cheer up. We Meadows women are made from hearty stock. Now I know why you turned down working for Kent. Time spent away from that cutie would not be recovered." She released her and joined the others.

Belinda didn't have time to linger on her thoughts. Ronald stood facing her with his intense brooding stare. "How soon do you plan to work with adults?"

"Right now, I'm focusing on children. I'm hoping that in a couple years we can expand. I don't want to rush things."

He nodded. In the same tight-lipped voice, he continued, "Our mother suffered from multiple sclerosis. She had various treatments, some drugs and rehabilitation. But she would have loved this. At the time, we were too young to know about this. Our father was focused parenting from afar." For the first time, a smile, sad and dreamy, appeared. "Our mother died on this day, last year."

Everything that Ronald said about his mother pierced her heart with the profound sadness around a lingering illness and the inevitable loss.

"We want to donate enough for you to open it up for the adults."

"I appreciate that. Let me think about it." When he didn't budge, she added, "Please."

He nodded. Then he turned and headed off in his own direction for his quiet inspection.

The one thing that was clear about the people drawn to the riding program was the common bond of knowing someone who needed the service. Of course, her connection with Maritza led her to Isabella and Dimitri's riding program. Given the large number of people in need, whether they had physical or emotional challenges, there weren't enough programs in existence. But that didn't mean that she should run out and build a program that was too large for her to manage. Plus she knew there would be a learning curve. No matter how much she planned, there would be potholes of various sizes and depths that would test her commitment. She had to go at her own pace.

At the end of the tour, Milton huddled with his siblings outside of the stable. Belinda had offered her office, but the urgency of their discussion couldn't seem to wait until they got back to the barn.

"Is there a problem?" the familiar deep voice asked behind her. "I did answer all their questions."

Belinda spun around, a bit rattled from Jesse's sudden comment, but also from his proximity. She licked her lips. She sorely needed water for the sudden dryness.

"They liked what they saw. Thank you." Belinda walked away, dismissing him with a flip of her hair.

"That was cold," Dana remarked, sounding like an annoying voice of conscience.

"Not really. Call it businesslike."

"That's what you're going to pretend is going on." Dana snorted. "Both of you are circling each other, testing each other's limits, pretend snarling, so attracted to each other that you can't stand it."

Belinda waved her off. Even if the siblings weren't done talking among themselves, they were now her target. It was either that or listen to more of Dana's unwanted advice.

"Ah…Belinda, we were going to talk to you." Milton took up the lead position for the family.

Belinda secretly hoped that the O'Hares mutually felt Ronald's excitement to be a donor.

"We are definitely interested in the program. We will donate our funds through the foundation in our mother's name. An official amount and the details with the donations will be forthcoming."

"Thank you." She was still blown away at the ease of getting the donation, although she wasn't sure what it meant, that they would provide her details with the donation. She or her program weren't for sale.

Dana hugged her after they wrapped up additional details. Belinda headed back in the stables and went into the stall for her favorite horse, Lucky Ducky. She led him out of the stall, saddled him for the ride and put on her helmet. She stuck her left foot into the stirrup and hoisted herself up as her right foot sailed over the back of the horse into the other waiting stirrup.

"Will you need to talk to me? I'm planning to leave at four thirty." It was Jesse.

Belinda leaned forward and stroked the horse's neck. It jiggled its long neck at her touch. The skin rippled under her strokes and her strong pats earned her a nod.

"Belinda, don't ignore me."

"Ignore? You're a fine one to bring up ignoring." The horse sidestepped toward the gate. Its eagerness to get out and into the ring increased its excitability. "What do you want from me, Jesse? It's pretty damn obvious that you're stalling in this game."

"Stalling? This may be a game to you, but it never was for me. And I didn't think you had a problem with the rules. You put them out there. So let me know exactly what part of the rules you want to change. I'm getting whiplash from my status of worker to lover and back to worker."

"I haven't changed a thing." She tempered her voice to keep the nervous horse in check. "But you could call. Text."

"Like a boyfriend would do." He held her wrist, stopping her in midstroke of the horse's neck. "Is that what I am to you? Maybe you should think about changing a few things." He stepped back, his mouth grimly set.

Belinda heard and felt the challenge. The pressure set her pulse racing. Fight or flight?

She clicked her tongue and squeezed her heels for the horse to go. Once the horse walked past Jesse and into the bright outdoors, Belinda continued into the ring for a warm-up before changing her cues, at which point Lucky Ducky responded, shifting into a gallop. She settled in to enjoy the rigorous ride. Her admission had been coerced by those gray eyes that pinned her for an answer that she really didn't want to give.

Now her wish had to come out in the open. But then what?

She gave Lucky Ducky the freedom to leave the ring and to head for the open field. The horse widened its stride and pushed forward. He wanted to be in the open, to run hard and burn off the energy. Belinda understood the feeling. The harsh pounding of the hooves vibrated throughout her body. Every part of her had to be engaged to stay on the horse and to participate in its exercise. In life, every part of her was scared to engage. And yet, a tiny *yes* wanted to escape out of her mouth. The admission released pent-up anxiety, a natural signal also to Lucky Ducky to shift down to a trot. Her cheeks stung with exhilaration.

Jesse hadn't left. He leaned against the fence of the riding ring, waiting for her return. His face was partially shaded under a hat, but she could feel his gaze locked on her movements. She aimed the horse toward him.

"Yes, Jesse Santiago, I want you to be my boyfriend," she said.

Belinda greeted her cousins with big hugs and kisses on their cheeks. Getting together was difficult. When they called her to come over, eat pizza and get her nails done, she jumped on it.

"Did you put a tint in your hair?" Belinda was truly amazed at Dana's transformation that didn't seem to slow down.

"Yes. Like it? Kind of auburn."

"Looks more golden brown than red brown." Fiona circled her, looking and touching Dana's new do.

"I like it," Dana declared. "Brings out my eyes."

"Sounds like something Kent said," Fiona teased. "Where is The Man?"

"Behind you." A familiar British accent shocked them into silence. "Maybe if I'd stayed quiet a tad longer, I would have heard what you really thought of me." He chuckled at their obvious discomfort.

Belinda's ears were hot. "Sorry."

"Nothing to apologize for." He hugged her and Fiona. "But I'm not going to stick around because I don't want to make you feel that you can't talk about me or my gender." He kissed Dana fully on the mouth. "Although my presence may not stop you."

"We speak the truth." Fiona wasn't going to do the backpedal like Belinda.

"Yeah, sure you do." Kent winked at Dana who gushed over his remarks like a schoolgirl.

"See you later." Her young cousin escorted her man to the door.

"I know they are committed to each other and all that, but I really do think that they're together...like forever."

Belinda nodded. "Feels good, doesn't it? We're growing up." The next phase of life about settling down, marriage and children seemed far away for Belinda. Her focus was now firmly homed in on her career as an equine-therapy specialist and all that it involved.

Dana returned and flopped into a nearby chair. "We're actually together...in the flesh."

"Can't believe it. Why are we so busy?" Belinda asked, already aware of the answer. They were all knee- or waist-deep in their careers. They had jobs that demanded more than the regular workday or workweek.

"I can't wait for us to have a spa day," Fiona moaned.

"We need to set the day and do it before we keel over from exhaustion." Belinda suffered more sleepless nights as the project got under way and she and Jesse never returned to their weekday arm's length and then weekend lovers-in-bed routine. Now her phone pinged throughout the day with their flirtatious texts, so at least that was something. Tonight, after she had let him know that she'd be with her cousins, she had turned off her phone. Otherwise, her cousins would forcibly take it from her and proceed to text on her behalf.

They threw out possible dates and discussed the merits of each as they divided the pizza and chomped on every juicy piece.

"You know, I have to say this." Dana finished chewing. "I'm proud that you are on the verge of opening the center."

It had been three weeks since Dana escorted the O'Hares, who not only wrote a starter check, but also pledged to donate a generous amount each year. In return, the stable would bear the name of their mother, while the Dreamweaver Riding Program name would remain intact. Belinda had no problem with that proposal.

However, she had to remain steadfast to her goals to service children, and later to expand to adults. Thankfully, Ronald accepted her plans, both short-term and long-term.

"Yeah. It's cool that opening day is around the corner," Fiona agreed.

"Stop making me sad," Belinda protested, although her heart was full of joy. Her cousins' approval meant so much to her because they knew each other so well.

Dana polished off a second slice before holding up a sauce-stained finger. "Now, don't get mad. But I don't think that you should have the grand opening without inviting Maritza."

"What?" Belinda almost choked on her pizza. "Maritza? I don't talk… She doesn't talk to me." She looked over to Fiona for help.

"I agree with Dana."

"Lately, you've been a real pain," Belinda groused.

"That's my new job in our happy trio. Listen, you always said Maritza inspired you to open the center." Fiona paused for Belinda's nod. "Then how can you not have her at the opening?"

"Did you both forget that Maritza isn't talking to me? She's mad at me. Hell, I'm mad at me."

"Time heals. If she doesn't make the first move, then you should." Fiona wasn't letting up.

"You suck." Belinda pointed at Fiona. "And you." She jabbed her finger at Dana.

"Now that you've got that out of your system, I did some digging and found her."

Belinda grabbed a slice of pizza and shoved her mouth full. The simple act stopped her from cursing.

"She's on this site. You can friend her. I did."

"You!"

"Me, too." Dana also helped herself with another slice. "She doesn't say much online. Lots of motivational quotes."

"Anything on forgiveness?" Belinda snipped. She hung her head, ashamed those words came out of her mouth. Her friend had every reason to be angry and to hold on to the beast.

Dana tapped her computer tablet and brought up the site. Their heads huddled together as the latest status updates popped into view. With a few more touches to the screen, the face of Maritza Carnegie smiled back at her. "We can take a look at her photos."

"Why did she accept your friend request? Does she know you're my cousin?" Belinda scanned the small number of photos. Could the measure of a life be held down to several photos? What she saw didn't tell her much, except that Maritza had emerged on-line in the past six months.

"She doesn't know." Fiona shrugged. "If she did, well, it's even better. Means that she's found her happy place."

"There is no happy place. She's in a wheelchair." Belinda held up her hand. "I did not just say it."

"Yeah, you did." Dana leaned over and popped her on the forehead. "Now I am more than certain that what we are doing is the right thing."

"Self-pity. Self-righteous. Patronizing." Fiona counted off on her fingers. "You need to get that taken care of before you open any center for people with challenges." She opened her pocketbook and pulled out a small piece of paper. "Here. Your assignment."

"And you can't say no," Dana ordered. Her hand poised for another forehead slap. "If you haven't figured it out, this is an intervention."

"What is my assignment?" Belinda took the paper and read Fiona's scrawl. "This is an address. You got her address."

"Wasn't hard." Fiona's smile had all her pride.

"Go to her, Belinda. Listen. Talk. Share. Forgive."

"She wasn't feeling me after the accident. I wrote. I called. I even visited for several years. Then the letters started coming back to me with a note from her parents that I was upsetting Maritza. That I was reminding her of her loss." Belinda stopped as the emotions surged with a full onward dive to sorrow.

"That's even more to talk about." Fiona scooted over and rested her arm on her shoulders.

"I'm not going to meet her." Belinda held up the

paper. She scrunched it and set it down next to her dirty napkins.

"Can't believe your heart is so hard." Dana pulled the almost-empty pizza box from her reach. "She's local. Go today."

"I know you want to see her. You must want to catch up and reminisce."

"Between you and her, you've got the world all figured." Belinda stood. "I hope this scenario was one that you figured on, because I'm leaving." She pushed away from the table. Without another word or a backward glance, she got her pocketbook and retrieved the keys. "I'm going home."

"Stubborn." Both cousins echoed their exact thoughts.

Belinda didn't like being blindsided. This wasn't a prank. This was her life. *Hers*. They just couldn't go marching into her life, trying to rearrange what they felt was broken. She jingled her keys and finished, "Let's take a break from the next meet-up. You all have killed the buzz for a while."

Thankfully, neither one reached out to stop her. She got in her car and sat for a few seconds. Maritza had returned to their hometown. How long ago had she been right under her nose? She banged the heel of her hand against the steering wheel. What the heck did she care where Maritza lived?

The drive home couldn't be fast enough. The cousins could wish for her to go to Maritza's house all they wanted, but she wasn't going on the hunt for her former friend. She had gotten used to saying that their friendship was over. But to reach out meant revisiting and revealing how hurt she had been that Maritza and her family had shut her out. Motivational quotes posted online on a status bar didn't mean there would be a thaw in their relationship.

Her hands curled tightly around the steering wheel. Tears seared her lids, both hot and angry. One day she was going to fix this. One day. The cousins had a knack for causing chaos. But she wasn't about to let it happen. She pulled into her driveway and parked in the garage.

Home. That's where she planned to be. Not on a mission to the unknown. She exited the car and stormed into the house, dropping her keys on the side table near the door. She reached in her pockets to empty the contents. A small, tightly balled paper came out with the loose change. Slowly, she unfurled the paper and saw Fiona's familiar handwriting.

Once again, she studied the address. Fiona must have slipped the paper in her pocket. She set down the paper on the counter and headed for the fridge to get water. Regardless of what Fiona or Dana said, she wasn't going anywhere today. Or tomorrow.

Unfortunately, an hour later, she couldn't stop thinking about that paper. Maritza. Their last conversation. She lay across the bed, staring at the small framed picture of her friend. This one was of them at a college fraternity dance. Its place was on the second shelf of the bookcase. Tucked away but still visible to her eye. A constant reminder of a friend that had walked out the door of her life and never returned.

Her phone buzzed with a text message. She sighed and pushed up to retrieve her phone. I'm here for you.

She typed back: Ok. Thx, Jesse.

Thank me in person. Open the door.

Belinda pushed off the bed and hurried to the door.

"What are you doing here?" She looked at him and then over his shoulder. "Is something wrong?" She couldn't help sounding so confused.

"I'm fine. Checking in with you." He stepped past her before she remembered to show a bit of hospitality.

"Checking on me? Why?"

"Figured you might be down. Wasn't sure how the meeting went with your friend…Maritza?"

"You know? How?" Belinda wished the fog would clear from her mind. After a trying day, she couldn't make sense of anything.

Jesse pulled her into his chest. "Don't get mad. Fiona called me, told me about Maritza, about how upset you were. That you were going to talk to your friend. But they hadn't heard from you."

"They kept calling. Pushing." Now it was her time to push, as she stepped away from Jesse's embrace. "I don't know what they expected."

"They wanted you to reach out to your friend—"

"Stop it. Just stop." She turned and walked into her bedroom. "The soft touch…whispery talk. I'm not a patient." Then she turned on him as the impact of what they'd done sank in. "It was none of your business." She sat on the edge of the bed.

Despite her harsh behavior, Jesse didn't leave. Instead, he slowly walked into the room without talking. For a few seconds, he stood, as if waiting for a read on her. She kept her eyes downcast on her hands, although she could also see his feet. "You helped me to forgive myself with Diego. I want to help you with your friend."

Her anger melted. "Maritza and I were close. Like sisters. The car accident wouldn't have happened if I had taken over the driving, like we'd planned. Instead, I let her do a double shift because I was tired, and so was she. And, well, I walked away. She didn't."

Jesse sat next to her. Gently he took her hand and held it between his.

"I went to the hospital every day. When she could talk, she didn't want to talk to me." She looked up at him. "I was all right with that. More than our bodies got banged up that day."

"Regardless of the past, you are doing what's right with the riding center. That counts for something."

Belinda sighed. "I had stopped visiting. I grew tired of being turned away because she didn't want to see me. But I didn't know when she was being discharged. When the guilt got to be too much, I went to visit, determined to see her regardless of what she said. Too late, she was discharged. Then I went to her parents. They wouldn't let me in."

"Oh, baby, sounds like everyone was hurting."

"Everyone blamed me."

"Yourself included?" He kissed her softly on the head.

"Just because Fiona and Dana got involved with stuff that didn't concern them, I'm supposed to do something about it."

"You don't have to."

Belinda took a deep breath and exhaled. She scooted back onto the bed and resumed her original position she had occupied before Jesse arrived. "I'll think about it."

His hand rested on her foot, stroking the slope leading up to her ankle.

"I can't be on someone's schedule. Just can't." Seeing Maritza wasn't the problem. It never was. Her rejection was the stab wound that hadn't healed. The best way to avoid that door slamming in her face was not to put herself in the same position.

Jesse scooted up alongside her. "You'll know when the time is right for you. Speaking from experience. It's a moment that you have to determine."

"When did you get cozy with my cousins?"

"Fiona called me. I thought you gave her my number."

"Good heavens, no."

"She called. Grilled me. Threatened and then—"

"Threatened?" Belinda propped herself on her elbow. She didn't know if she should wring Fiona's neck or hug her for being the overprotective cousin.

"Let's see. She said that she was a detective and knew how to hide bodies. That Grace could fund any size manhunt if I should harm you. And Dana added her input that she could destroy me in the media." Jesse kissed her breast. "If I had any inclination to the dark side, I think they scared me straight."

"After she threatened you, what happened?"

"Then she told me that you had some heavy stuff to deal with regarding Maritza. I didn't ask any questions. I'd rather hear it from you. But when she suggested that I come and check in on you, I didn't object at all."

"Glad you came over. I'm impressed by your sensitive side. Makes me like you more."

He kissed the tip of her nose. "Sometimes it's buried from lack of use. But it's my pleasure."

Belinda closed her eyes and surrendered to Jesse's touch that magically stroked away the worry.

Chapter 10

Friday morning rolled in with a sonic fury. A series of thunderclaps snapped Belinda awake. Her heart raced as her foggy brain tried to figure out what happened. Jagged streaks of lightning lit up the gray morning. Another crash of thunder blasted away any sleepy remnants of confusion. Her hand blindly reached behind her for Jesse. No one was there. Empty, cold sheets gathered under her fingers.

She cracked an eyelid open to peer at the clock. Ten o'clock! She bolted up and grabbed her phone. It lay silent and dark. It was dead because she forgot to hook it up to the charger. After it got some juice, she saw that Tawny and Fiona had called. Her mouth pursed with a curse ready to spring. A night's sleep hadn't erased her indignation over what her cousins had done.

Finally, Belinda mustered enough energy to get out of bed. When she finally listened to Tawny's voice message, it was her assistant reminding her that she was taking the day off. Luckily, there were no appointments, but she could be happy that three clients had signed up. With her total customer roll hovering at fifteen, she considered it a good start. Now Jesse had to pull through with an on-time delivery. One thing was for sure—he could deliver on time, every time, in her bed. She smiled and drew the bed linens around her, enjoying the lingering smell of him and their passionate night.

Still, he hadn't shared what was on his mind. He'd lowered the fence for her and her problems, but remained quietly troubled by whatever kept that sadness in place in his body. Taking one day at a time, she had to trust that he would see her in the light of a best friend, confidante, his personal cheerleader.

She'd made headway with the paperwork she needed filed when there was a knock at the office door. Since Tawny wasn't there, and the workers weren't in earshot, she'd locked the entrance to give herself peace of mind. Besides, Tawny had said there were no appointments.

The security monitor showed Dana pacing in front of the entrance. Belinda stared at it for a few seconds, debating her cousin's entry and enjoying Dana's impatience.

Finally, she opened the door. "What do you want, Dana? I'm busy."

"I came to apologize."

"A phone call would have sufficed. Even an email." Belinda didn't invite Dana to her office. She remained standing in the lobby area with her hip resting against the file cabinet.

Dana hung her head. Then she parked a coaxing smile on her face. "Hugs?"

"Come one step closer and I'm going to punch your arm."

"What?" Dana straightened up and erased the smile. "Okay, so we overstepped. You don't have to get hostile."

"Why would you involve Jesse? That's way beyond overstepping."

"I like him. I think he'd be great for you. And… since it seemed that you had a falling out with him, we thought that it would be a heroic thing for him to show up after you visited Maritza."

"You're going to make me cuss." Belinda stared at her cousin. "Then I'm going to kick your behind."

"I'm a CEO. I'll call security on you."

"Well, when you limp your silly butt back to your fancy car, you can call in the cavalry. I'm so mad that I'll kick their behinds, too." Belinda expected such high-handed behavior from her grandmother. But this level of manipulation from her cousins floored her. "And then…and then, to use Jesse to save me." Now she had to walk in the small area. "Save me."

Dana ignored her rant. "Did you go see Maritza?"

"No."

"Instead of getting indignant about what I did… yes, you have all rights." Dana retreated to the door when Belinda stopped her pacing. "Remember this was about the opening of the center. And her. And you. A friendship."

The reminder was worse than Jesse's reminder of what she'd done for him after he made up with Diego.

"It's time. It's long overdue." Dana approached with arms outstretched. "And I can't have my fave cousin be mad at me for one more minute."

Belinda pulled her into a bear hug. For her ultimate revenge, she held her tightly and tousled Dana's pinned-up hairdo before releasing her. "Okay, I feel better. Now get out of my office."

"Now I'm going to have to go back to the hairdresser. You just don't like to see people looking better than you and that old-fashioned ponytail." Dana huffed her way out of the office. But their skirmish had evaporated under their laughter.

There was no way that she could return her attention to the work on her desk. She pulled out the paper with Maritza's information and debated whether to call or show up. Both had their risks. At the moment, she was more focused on what could go wrong than what could go right.

Breakfast wasn't on the agenda. After a sleepless night, and a slow roll out of bed, Belinda preferred sipping on herbal tea. If her stomach wasn't so queasy, she'd opt for something stronger. Since her cousins had been chewed out, they weren't going to jump at the chance to accompany her. And her stubborn nature wouldn't allow her to ask them to come. Something else stopped her…a touch of fear.

Belinda sent a short note that morning to Maritza, as she sipped on herbal tea at her desk, and the note had not been answered. Instead of mailing it, she'd used the email address listed in the profile of the friend site.

Maritza, it's been some time since we last saw each other. Hoping that I can meet with you soon. Looking forward to hearing from you.

Three sentences that took an hour and half to write, then another thirty minutes for her to reflect and keep her index finger close to the delete key.

She drained the cup of cooling tea. No more delays.

Jesse wasn't the type to hunt down his women. On more than one occasion, he was the hunted as he dodged many clingy females. Those days had faded so far into the recesses of his past since he arrived, since he'd met Belinda, that he never once looked back or pined for those days. While he was ready to move ahead, the timing wasn't right. Holding back, holding her off, until he figured out his life was the only path. It hurt like hell. But he'd done enough hurt and damage that his pain was nothing. That's why he now lay in an empty bed staring at his phone, waiting for a response to his many calls and texts to Belinda.

His doorbell rang. He pulled on a T-shirt over his pajama bottoms and hurried to the door.

"Belinda, come in." Jesse didn't mean to sound so surprised.

"I know you didn't expect me."

"Ah…no, it's okay. Make yourself comfortable." Seeing Belinda at his door shocked the heck out of him. Although they were tentatively trying out the boyfriend-girlfriend scenario, she had only accepted his invitations to his home a few times. At first, he didn't mind because it was convenient to have home and office on the same site when they wanted to shift things to a more intimate level. But now he wanted to be the one to entertain her on his turf.

He headed for the kitchen and pulled out water and a wine bottle. From her sudden appearance and markedly subdued attitude, he wasn't sure which one was needed tonight. He grabbed two wineglasses on his way to the living room.

"Guess it's a bit of surprise to see me here."

He shrugged and set down his offerings on the glass-top table.

"Life is weird." She took the water bottle.

He followed suit, waiting for an explanation to match the philosophical statement.

"Doing the right thing doesn't guarantee any rewards."

He waited.

"Making things right doesn't guarantee any rewards."

That statement, he could buy into.

"I visited Maritza."

"Oh." Now he set down the water bottle and filled a glass of wine for himself.

She looked up at him, the tears welling in her eyes. Her voice trembled with a breathy hitch.

Jesse squeezed into the single chair that she chose to sit in. He pulled her onto his lap. "Tell me what happened. You know that I would have gone with you."

Belinda shook her head. "It's too easy to lean on someone when this is all mine to handle." She nuzzled his chin with its five o'clock shadow.

"Tell me about it." This wasn't the time to be stubborn and force her to understand that he was here for the good and the not-so-good, even though he was keeping his growing dilemma to himself. He pulled her closer to his chest and leaned his head toward hers. "Tell me about Maritza."

Belinda closed her eyes, recalling what had recently transpired.

The Maritza she'd remembered in college wasn't the Maritza who coolly regarded her while sitting on the large wraparound porch of her house. Her college friend had been a bundle of energy, life of the parties, who always had a crowd around her. She had talent, winning competitions in college. She had brains and plans to go to law school. She was beautiful, inside and out.

Now there was an older version, quiet and mature. The impulsive energy was gone or turned inward. Belinda hadn't known what to expect. Part of her wanted her old friend back, before the accident, the way she remembered her.

It was a shock to pull up and see her there. She'd hoped to have time to compose herself at the door. Instead, what she'd wanted to say—her rehearsed speech—flew out of her mind.

Maritza had studied her with heavy suspicion before her face relaxed as recognition sunk in. Any courage that had stirred to life to get Belinda this far fled as her former friend coolly regarded her. Belinda had taken a retreating step when Maritza invited her to have a seat.

Belinda had started, *I sent you an email.*

I didn't want to respond.

So I came…unannounced. She'd sat on the wide railing with one of the support beams at her back.

Sorry. The apology had multiple uses, but at the time, Belinda had used it for the blindsided visit.

Not a problem.

I came...to find you. I wanted to invite you to... Belinda had wondered how everything that she'd planned to say had evaporated into the foggy mental mist. *I created a riding school called Dreamweaver Riding Program for children with disabilities and challenges.* Her voice had petered out and she'd cleared her throat to continue. *The grand opening is in a month. And I'd like for you to be there.*

I'm confused. Maritza had clasped her hands. *What does this have to do with me?*

Since the accident, I wanted to do something that could help children. Belinda had swallowed. *You inspired me.*

Maritza hadn't responded. She'd kept her gaze fastened on the slats. Then she'd taken a long, deep breath. Still she'd remained silent, unnerving Belinda.

I would love to invite you to the facility. To see what services the clients will receive.

Why would I want to see that?

It would be my way of saying sorry.

You could have said sorry many times. You could have done it at the hospital. At my home. When I was going to rehab. Although Maritza had spoken in a monotone, her words held enough anger to make a mark.

I reached out to you. I visited until I was told that you didn't want visitors. I came to your house until your parents said that you weren't coping well. The doctors said that you needed time to heal. Then I came back a month later and you were no longer living there. You and your parents were gone.

I wrote you.

I never got any letters. Belinda had sat next to her friend and tentatively taken her hand between hers. *I wanted to find you. But then it sunk in that you didn't want to be friends because of what I'd done.*

Done?

I should have been the one driving.

Maritza had looked away toward the street. A car had pulled into the driveway. A man emerged and assisted two children out from the back. *These are my husband and children.*

Wow! Belinda had needed a moment to regroup. All this time, she'd thought that Maritza was suffering from her wounds, possibly unable to go on, struggling to find the positive side of things. And here, in front of her, she was seeing her husband, son and daughter.

I've moved on, Belinda. It's clear that my parents manipulated us. They were angry and scared. You were the target. I'm sure that in feeling sorry for myself, I also blamed you. For that, I'm truly sorry.

After the brief introductions, Maritza had waited until her family went into the house. *I'm happy, Belinda. I would say I forgive you, but that would mean that I felt you did something wrong. You most certainly did not.* Then it had been Maritza's turn to clasp Belinda's hand. *And you? Your family? Any children?*

Belinda had shaken her head at each guess. All she'd focused on was the business and paying penance.

I think we can feel assured that neither of us owes the other a thing.

Belinda had nodded. Her throat felt thick, the lump in it rising, squeezing off the tears that were ready to fall.

Belinda came back to herself. "She was wrong, Jesse. We were like sisters. I want it all back."

Under the soft light of the lamp, Belinda sniffled softly as she told the final notes of the story of the long day. But she didn't want him to make a fuss—just to continue holding her within his arms. Holding her *and* loving her.

The phone rang. Jesse eased his arm from under Belinda's head. She had slept curled into his body after they made love.

He answered the phone after it rang, went to his voicemail, and then rang again. Curious and sleepily irritated, he pressed the talk button.

"Yes," he answered drowsily.

"Jesse, I hope that I didn't wake you. The time difference messes with my head. I'll be heading your way in a couple of days. Me and Arthur."

"Why are you and my agent coming to Midway? It's off the beaten path." Jesse still had a few outstanding contracts with advertisers. It was the only reason he still had Arthur. Frankly, there was no new business to be discussed.

"Stop being a grumpy old man." Olivier's exuberance was too much to handle.

"You interrupted my morning with a very beautiful woman."

"Really? Will I get to meet her?"

"Never."

"Uh…man. Not fair. Hope it's not too serious. You

know what I mean? You're rehabbing, not settling down or anything. I shouldn't have left you to your own devices for so long. You're getting domesticated on me."

"I'm hanging up, Olivier."

"Wait. Okay, maybe I need a woman in my life, too."

Jesse squeezed his eyes shut. Olivier was on his way out of marriage number four. The man truly seemed to be in love with the courtship through honeymoon phases. He was stuck on a repeat cycle, but emerged with more energy than when he went into the relationship.

"Like I said, we'll be there soon. Can't wait for you to get out of there and get your life back on track."

"Don't rush." Jesse hung up the phone and sighed. Any remnant of sleep disappeared. He looked back at Belinda and she was awake, watching him.

"You're okay?"

He nodded.

"They want you back."

"Yeah." He pushed off the bed and put on clothes. "Breakfast?"

"No. I'm good. Gotta head to the office."

Jesse knew that Belinda wanted to talk, ask him questions, delve into what his feelings were. But he couldn't go there. Not even her disappointment could make him voice the increasing turmoil over his new reality. What would he do after the project ended? His read on Belinda wasn't clear about if they'd continue on when he no longer had work-related tasks to bring them together.

Being close to her, staying in the town, enjoying each other in this temporary, fleeting way had been exciting and addictive. *Had.* Now the sensations shifted into worrisome doubt. The second-guessing turned him back toward soccer, as an option he reluctantly entertained. But the longer he stayed in this state of limbo, the deeper the permanent pain was of not having Belinda. Soon they would have nothing in the middle between them to tie them to each other.

Belinda hugged him from behind, pressing her naked body against his back. "Don't block me out."

He shook his head. "This was supposed to be easy. It wasn't going to be..."

"A big deal." She took a deep breath as she rested her cheek against his warm skin. "It's not. We agreed that we could walk away at any time without drama." She walked around him and knelt at his knees. The dark unrest on his face saddened her. Her heart swelled heavy with dread for the incoming tide that would change everything. Whenever Olivier called, she sensed Jesse's constant retreat from her. She wished that she could block the calls. One thing that she knew for sure was that Jesse was happy. From the man who was surly at their first meeting, to this man who said all the right things when she was curled in his arms, he had found peace. But his old mistress— soccer—wasn't ready to let go. Maybe Olivier sensed that in his conversations with Jesse. Hence, the daily check-in. Belinda felt the clock ticking on her own happiness.

"Let's live in the moment. For however long," Belinda suggested with a lie.

"You know that couples always say that and then

it doesn't go as planned. Someone doesn't adhere to the rules."

Belinda eased away from him. One thing that she had learned of Jesse was his renewed desire to keep his life in organized slots. Nice and neat. Predictable and comfortable. "Last time, you changed our status."

"Yeah, and you agreed."

Belinda wagged her index finger at him. "This time, I'll propose the change—"

"Uh-oh."

"And I'm thinking that some rules may need tweaking. Right now, we are not on the same playing field."

"To play?" His forehead creased with deep furrows. His eyes attempted to pierce through her cavalier demeanor.

"That's what we're doing. We play. We have fun. As long as we don't cross the borders." She pushed him onto his back, rose from her knees and comfortably straddled his hips. His arousal grew under her, taunting with its thickness.

"Following rules sucks." His voice thickened. Desire showed in his eyes.

Belinda turned her attention to Jesse's magnificent body. She slid her hand along the length of his right thigh up toward his scar that went over his hip and curved around his back. He never wanted her to touch the long incisions.

"Today, I'm changing the rules." Gently, Belinda's fingers traced the thick line left by the scalpel's cut. The old wound didn't offend her. She was more interested in the new injuries tearing through his willpower that she knew were there.

He gritted his teeth, sucking in air. His hand shot out and imprisoned hers.

"I touch you." She leaned forward inches from his face. "And you can touch me wherever you like."

"I'm not budging."

She used her other hand and slid it along his other thigh. The muscles contracted and twitched under her fingers.

"I can resist." His hiss sounded labored.

Taking his hand, she guided it to her sex.

"Wicked woman," he whispered.

She bit her lip to stifle her own groans. But she couldn't help the long series of breathy moans when his fingers delivered a sensual massage between her legs. Her thighs squeezed together. Spasms jerked her body as he slid his fingers in her. She held on to him like a rollercoaster, although this ride was steadily heading to dizzying heights with no sign of letting up. That heady sense of hitting the top layers of ecstasy revved her hunger. Slick with her juices, his fingers fed her needs. In and out. Slow and steady until she ground her hips, squeezing and urging him to go deep and hard. On that fine edge, she mounted, ready to let go and take the plunge into ecstasy. Her climax took the wind out of her lungs as she arched back. Free-falling. Sailing. Floating.

"Negotiations over," she whispered, before sliding off his body. *And I love you with all my heart.*

Chapter 11

Jesse pulled into his parents' driveway, still unsure if bringing Belinda was a good idea. His parents and Diego demanded that they meet her. Never had he brought home anyone. Considering the women he met during his sporting days, no one had gotten close enough for any official meetings. Today being a day of firsts, he was worried that they would press beyond what he could handle.

Dammit, he loved her. Something no one would guess, particularly his mother, who had a knack for discovery.

Now he dared to consider a future with Belinda, rather than remaining on the sidelines. The more he fell for Belinda, the more that he wanted things his way and to have it all. The fall into deep love was a long tumble and he wasn't sure if he'd reached the bottom. Losing control freaked him out. Every min-

ute of the day, he thought about Belinda. Calling
her on the phone just to hear her voice and enjoy the
light rumble of her laughter. Teasing her about the
goofy selfies that she constantly sent to his phone.
Every waking second, thoughts of her fed his craving. When his head hit the pillow at night, she filled
his dreams and his fantasies. More than once, he'd
awakened aroused and aching for intimate, sensual
contact with her body.

If he continued with this free fall, he'd lose himself. Never having experienced such intense passion
before, he couldn't decide if it was healthy or dangerous. Relying on feelings alone, he'd say that his
headfirst pitch over the edge had him fighting for his
breath, seeking oxygen. Nothing else mattered. Selfish, his brother had once called him. How fitting the
label. Yes, he was truly self-focused.

"Jesse, we're here." Belinda interrupted his musings.

Taking a deep breath, Jesse stepped out and
rounded the car to open Belinda's door.

"Stop looking so nervous." She took his offered
hand and exited.

"This seemed like a good idea at the time, last
week," he muttered.

His mother opened the front door and stepped out
with her arms open—for Belinda. Jesse got a glare
and a pursed mouth for his delay in introducing her
to his family. He followed his mother and Belinda
locked arm in arm into the house.

The heavenly smell of dinner greeted him warmly.
At least he could tend to the cold shoulder with a
healthy serving of good food.

"How's it going so far with Mom and Belinda? By the way, I like her," Diego whispered.

"The South Pole is on a thaw."

"Diego, how are you doing? Come sit down." Caroline turned to Jesse. "Get your father a glass of water. Why are you standing there doing nothing?" She fretted some more while Diego was coddled and made comfortable in the family room.

Meanwhile, Belinda was chatting with his father. Smiles and laughter galore.

On his way to the fridge, he caught Diego's smug expression. Jesse shook his head and got busy with his task. Regardless of his mother's pretension at being disgruntled, the fact was that everyone had fallen for Belinda; for them, that was a real sign that he was settling down and moving on with his life.

Later his father started the meal with a heartfelt prayer. Jesse bowed his head and offered his own prayer of gratitude. He raised his head at the end of his father's close and took a deep breath to settle his chaotic thoughts.

"Let's dig in." Ed started carving the roast and handed it out as plates were passed his way.

"Mom, everything smells delicious." Jesse tried a step onto the thin ice. "I remember that you'd make the scalloped potatoes when I got *A*s." He grinned with what he hoped was his cherubic five-year-old spirit.

Caroline sniffed, but her face softened as she looked at him. "I even brought it to you at the soccer camp."

"Oh, that must have been priceless," Belinda added.

"I got teased a lot for that." Those days were filled with anticipation and dreams of a professional athlete's life.

"And you worked harder than all those guys to get to the top," Ed reminded.

"It's still there for you," Belinda suggested with a gentle touch.

Only the sound of silverware hitting the plates could be heard.

"Belinda, that's noble of you, but I think that train has left the station." Diego raised his water glass to her.

Jesse switched topics. "So, what's the news on the medical front for Dad?"

"Oh, yes," Caroline looked at her husband. "There is one artery partially blocked. They are talking about putting in a stent to prop open its walls."

"I don't think those doctors know anything. I feel fine," his father protested.

"One of my aunts has had the procedure. It's not as invasive as surgery," Belinda provided.

Diego nodded.

"Dad, go ahead and get it done. Don't rush it," Jesse urged. "I've got everything covered. You don't have to think about anything. Diego and I have things in control."

"Enough with my health issues." Ed got up and started clearing away the dishes. "And you, Jesse, stop sitting there making goo-goo eyes at Belinda. Help clear the table and load the dishwasher."

Belinda popped up next to him. "I'll help." She took several dishes to the kitchen despite the all-around protests.

His father headed to the pantry to get more dish-washing liquid. Jesse took the opportunity to lean toward Belinda. "You didn't have to pretend to clean away the dishes to be next to me."

She poked him in the ribs. "Why would I possibly want to get near you?"

"Because you wanted a chance to feel this." He kissed her shoulder. It twitched. "And a chance for me to do this." He kissed the back of her neck. She hunched her shoulders. "But most of all, you wanted me to play the bad guy." His hand rested on her hip as he kissed the edge of her ear. His tongue traced the graceful curve of the delicate coil. Her body shud-dered against the frame of his. Without a doubt, she was as turned on as much as he was. He couldn't wait to bring the evening to an end. Other matters required his attention. His hand that rested on her backside slid to grip her hip.

"I didn't find the dishwashing liquid. Don't worry about it. You can load the dishwasher." Ed walked into the kitchen holding a bottle of detergent as he tried to read the small print.

"That's for clothes, Ed." Belinda's hand slid out of Jesse's grasp so smoothly and quickly that he couldn't help but laugh. His chuckling earned him a glare from her while his dad did his best to read the label with-out his reading glasses.

"Pop, we've got this. Why don't you go chat with Diego?" He added, "Save him from Mom."

"You're right." His father allowed Belinda to re-lieve him of the detergent and left the room.

"Together at last," Jesse teased. His laughter sounded as wicked as he could muster.

"I'm not playing with you, Mr. Santiago. We are in your parents' house."

"You don't think they hugged and kissed back in the day, and more so now that the house is empty?" Jesse suddenly spun her toward him. "Like this?" Nothing mattered, except to hold her in his arms. As she opened her mouth to protest, he covered her sweet lips with his.

"Jesse," she whispered against his mouth, which earned her another kiss. "Your mother may come in."

"I think they know we're dating."

She planted a quick kiss and gave him a decisive push. "I'll wash. You load."

"Okay. But then can we go back to hugging and kissing?"

"You are beyond help."

He grinned. "Don't your parents get busy in their kitchen?"

"Thank goodness, I didn't have to witness it if they did." Belinda began washing off the dishes before handing them to Jesse.

Dishes were loaded. The counter was cleaned. Food was put away in the refrigerator. Evidence of the large meal had disappeared. Jesse followed Belinda into the family room.

"Belinda, sit next to me. Let's look at Jesse's baby pictures."

Jesse was suddenly abandoned by Belinda when she plopped down next to Diego.

"Oh my, you're in a little wash basin." Belinda flashed him the photo. There he sat in water that barely covered his hips in a large basin that his mother converted into his personal tub.

"I've got more photos," Caroline exclaimed and left the room.

"Why are we looking at my photos anyway?" Jesse protested.

His mother returned with bundles of pictures.

"Mom, you really should get those scanned," Diego suggested.

Caroline shushed him. "Diego was our artist in residence. First the violin. Trumpet."

"Drums," Ed added and shook his head.

"Were you good?" Belinda looked over at his brother.

"He was great." Jesse didn't mind bragging about him. He'd managed to see him once when he played at a nightclub.

"We were going to start a band. Jesse would play rhythm guitar and I would play drums. We had posted signs for band members around the neighborhood."

"Really? How old were you?" Belinda asked.

Jesse saw the accusation in Belinda's playful scowl that he hadn't shared this juicy bit.

"I was ten. Jesse was sixteen," Diego volunteered.

"What happened to the band?" Belinda pointed her curiosity at Diego.

"The soccer team came knocking. It was Jesse's time to step up." His brother spoke with quiet pride that still had the effect of embarrassing Jesse.

"Everything has its time in the sun before moving on." Jesse did his best to deflect any further discussion.

"Does that include people, too?" Belinda asked.

"Don't ask him that question," Diego warned. "I

think my brother thinks that it's weak to rely on some-one."

"Stop spreading nonsense. We all live according to our phases and chapters in life. Every new experi-ence is a new chapter to look forward to."

"Belinda, you have a smart man on your hands."

"I know. I'm a lucky woman."

While his mother applauded over the romantic dec-laration, his father leaned over to him and thumped his back.

Jesse gave a thumbs-up, although what he felt was hardly worthy of celebration.

A week later, Belinda didn't know why she al-lowed Dana to talk her into having a silent auction to coincide with the opening of the center. All day, the activities would roll out, beginning with the local mayor and city council cutting the ribbon and mak-ing their speeches.

A small army of workers had arrived earlier and built the stage and set for the ambience. She had to admit that the circus theme looked impressive and of-fered the right tone. The large posters of horses and child models were on display. On several monitors, videos played trailers about the program. Every de-tail had been planned.

"It's game time, kiddo." Fiona popped in her head through the bedroom door.

"Hey, didn't think you were coming." Belinda hugged her cousin. "Thought you had to work."

"I did, but I set it aside." She lightly touched her cheek. "This is your day. We celebrated Dana's rise to the job of her heart and now we celebrate yours. So let's go."

Belinda nodded.

"By the way, you are looking quite snazzy in this maxi dress."

"I went with bright colors. It should make everyone happy. Figured it might coax the folks to donate or sponsor the horses' training." Belinda slipped on a light jacket over the floor-length maxi. She wore a pair of white gladiator-style sandals with four-inch heels. As a first in a long time, she endured hours at a hairdresser's shop to have her hair professionally styled into ringlets down her back.

Despite what she wore to impress her guests and show Grace that she could clean up, on the inside, her nerves spiked up the chart and headed for a meltdown. Preparations, the few last-minute changes and natural game-day jitters gnawed at her. Today marked the end of a chapter of completing a portion of her vision. Instead of dancing a quick two-step in celebration, she saw that fear, brutally cold and ever-present, wanted in on the opening day to remind her that failing wasn't beyond her reach.

"You know…you did it." Fiona gave her hug.

"Some mornings, I can't believe that I've gotten this far."

"Your mom and stepdad arrived. I saw them talking to Grace."

"Good." She was pleased that they'd come. Her parents' relationship with her was more awkward than strained. For the most part, they stayed on their own turfs unless there was an official family event.

They headed toward the stables. A good crowd attended the festivities, further raising her spirit. She scanned the faces, many familiar, quite a few not. Everyone seemed to be mingling and enjoying the venue.

"Oh my…word." Fiona froze. Her gaze stayed directed on the tall man in front of them.

"Lionel, what are you doing here?" Belinda hadn't seen Lionel in months. And she'd rather not provide him with the incentive to bring up her past.

"Well, I didn't expect such a reception."

"You weren't invited." Belinda saw no need to be diplomatic. Lionel didn't operate well under innuendoes and subtle adjustments to tone of voice.

"I do have a donation that I'd like to make."

"You can leave it with Tawny."

"And, then…?" He hadn't stepped closer to her. Yet he used his body and build to send intimidating messages. Lionel had height, but he also carried a lot of weight. The thick stature had gotten him mistaken for a professional wrestler many times.

"And then nothing. I'll send you a thank-you gift." On that note, Belinda swept past him, leaving Fiona behind to close up the situation. She couldn't stand to be in his company any longer than necessary. The sound of his voice had a nasal twang that made her want to karate-chop his neck.

In no time, the crowd swallowed her, providing a natural barrier around her space. Soon it would be time for her to step up and deliver the opening speech, a ten-minute introduction on herself and the center to start things off. Poor Jesse had had to listen to various versions during the week. Maybe she should have chewed on a couple antacids this morning.

"Have you seen Jesse?" she asked Tawny, who was taking selfies with different guests.

"No. Did you need him for something?"

Belinda shook her head. "It's not that important."

She left Tawny with her task to scan the crowd for him. Hopefully, nothing had popped up to make him late.

"Time for your speech." Tawny had put away the cell phone. "Go wow these people. You're really doing something that has impact and longevity."

"You've been hanging around the politicians too long. But I thank you for the compliment on our efforts."

Fiona swooped in with Dana in tow. "You look ready to hurl. But I did get rid of one reason that would have made you hurl."

"Lionel." All three cousins called out the name together.

Belinda whined, "Why didn't I get one of you to make the speech?"

Fiona snorted.

"Because we want to see you grow."

"Dana, be quiet. Your suggestion could earn you an instant eviction off the premises. Tawny, stop giggling over there."

Belinda closed her eyes, took a deep breath to push back the nausea. It was showtime. On trembling legs, she walked toward the stage and then stepped onto the little staging area and approached the podium.

A small jazz ensemble stopped its playing of popular music. The crowd continued on with its activities as she stood on the stage, trying to get its attention.

Tawny snagged the audience's awareness with her piercing whistle.

Belinda shook her head to clear the aftereffects of the whistle. Everyone's focus turned toward her. From her vantage point, she could identify most of the guests. But right now she was only looking for Jesse. To see his approval would set the right tone for her. He could calm her, charm her and counsel her through so many of her highs and lows. *Jesse, where are you?*

She cleared her throat. Time to begin. Her gaze slid from the notes in her hand out to the back of the reception area. There he was. Her smile grew wider as he waved from his hiding spot off to the side. Two men stood behind him in suits that didn't blend with the rest of the guests. A cool shiver ran through her. She knew deep in her bones that it was Olivier and Arthur—Jesse's trainer and agent. They'd come as promised to entice Jesse back to soccer and back to Spain.

Belinda swallowed the thick swell of emotion and started her speech about her friendship with Maritza. She knew it was important that the guests understood who this special woman was, her dreams ahead and the sharp detour in her life.

She shared her feelings, touching on her guilt, but tying in the needs and benefits for the riding program. Her credit went out to mentors like Isabella and Dimitri, but she made sure to include her cousins and grandparents, especially Grace, for their support and hours of advice and hand-holding.

Finally, the wrap-up of the speech spotlighted the O'Hare family and its generosity. Singlehandedly, they had wiped away a lot of the financial burden to open on time. When the applause simmered down, she continued with her praise by mentioning how they were honoring their mother's memory with the unveiling of her name on the stable.

Flushed with embarrassment for her next action, Belinda took a deep breath and expressed in a big exhalation her admiration and gratitude to Jesse and his team for completing the impressive Dreamweaver Riding facility on time and on budget.

After the crowd applauded, she turned away from the podium. But Tawny barreled toward her with a huge grin and arms outstretched, preventing Belinda's exit from the stage. Her assistant leaned into the microphone. "Ladies and gentlemen, the woman who inspired this center."

The crowd murmured. Anticipation in the air buzzed like electricity.

Belinda looked at Tawny as if she'd lost her mind. Then she noticed the small family coming onto the platform. Maritza, with the aid of a cane, slowly walked the length of the stage. Her husband and children waited off to the side. Their pride and love were easily discernible.

"Thank you." Maritza, with tears streaming down her face, hugged her tightly.

"You came." Belinda didn't realize she was crying until Tawny pressed tissues into her hand.

"I'm so sorry for the way I treated you."

Belinda waved it off. "You're here. That means a lot."

Maritza stepped up to the podium and shared the tough emotional and physical journeys of rehabilitation, while lauding the importance of horse-assisted therapy facilities like Dreamweaver.

Belinda was proud of Maritza's story. As the event winded down, pieces of her speech resonated with her. Her friend was a survivor, not only in the literal sense, but in what she'd overcome. Once again, she had inspired Belinda to take charge, like with what she wanted, who she wanted guilt-free—Jesse.

Jesse stayed out of Belinda's way. This was his woman's big day. Nothing that brewed in his corner of life needed to mar this event. With Olivier and Arthur hovering like black crows, interjecting themselves in his world, he didn't want them anywhere near Belinda. To see and hear her engaging the audience's attention with a heartfelt speech filled him with love. He coughed, in a weak attempt to shake loose the strange, new emotion.

"You okay?" Tawny popped into his space, offering him a glass of generic punch that she lifted off a passing waiter.

"Thanks." He drained the glass, glad for the respite.

She whispered loudly, "Why are you in spy mode over here?"

"It's cooler. Lots more shade." The grand opening event filled the property around the renovated stable and along the road that led to the office. In that area, he stayed under the trees, keeping his companions out of the way. They had stepped aside from him to talk without his interference or input.

Tawny leaned in to him. "So, now that the work is done, will I be seeing you hanging around the office?"

He took a deep breath. "No. I think this job is all wrapped up."

"Oh, I see." Her eyebrows peaked in total disapproval.

Jesse wished that he could find another spot, away from Tawny's prying and out of sight of Olivier and Arthur. It certainly wasn't going to happen now. Belinda, with her beautiful hips swaying from side to side, headed directly toward him.

"Hey, baby." Belinda slid her arm through his and around his waist. "I almost had a heart attack when I didn't see you earlier." She turned his insides into gooey nonsense with her smile.

"I wouldn't have missed it. You were fantastic."

"Only fantastic?" She nuzzled his cheek.

He wanted to wrap his arms around her and not let go. "Way more than fantastic. Enthralling."

"Oh, I like it when you use three-syllable words." She sighed. "But I can't play right now. I've got to go mingle and do all that schmoozing. But you and I…later?"

"Okay." He kissed her forehead.

"Hey, what's the matter? I know that sad puppy look."

"Either you tell her or I will." Tawny squared off like an MMA fighter ready to charge. She had stepped in their space with hands on her hips. All her attention stayed on Jesse.

"What?" Belinda looked at her assistant and then at him.

"He's going to break up with you because Frick and Frack are here to take him away. Kidnap him, if necessary. Guess he was only out on parole."

"The pallbearers in the back?"

"They're not important to anything here," Jesse objected. "They came here straight from the airport because they'd just got off the plane."

Belinda glared at him, locking in her tracking beam of a gaze to his face, specifically his eyes. "Somehow I don't buy that there's nothing important going on." She turned at his colleagues. "Would you please introduce yourselves?"

"We're here to talk to Jesse. I'm Olivier and this is Arthur." Olivier had opted for a polite demeanor, while his agent must have figured his cheesy grin would work on Belinda.

"The soccer reapers have come for your soul, Jesse." Her tone could've had icicles dripping from each word.

"So it would seem." Tawny looked ready for a fight.

Belinda turned her attention to him. Hurt dimming the sparkle in her eyes. "Just like that, you're leaving. I know that Tawny doesn't blow things out of proportion. And she wouldn't say something that could snap my heart in two…on an important day of my life."

"They came bearing gifts to entice me back onto the field." He took her hand and held it. "I didn't say that I was breaking up with you." Jesse wished that he could press the rewind button. "I was saying that my job was done."

Tawny turned to Olivier and Arthur. "Let's go. Now. Let them be."

Belinda continued, "From anyone else, I'd take it at face value." She patted away the tears and backed away from him. "You don't break up. You just remove yourself from lives. Mine."

Jesse didn't like the accuracy of her aim. "I lied."

"About what?"

"I can't pretend that I don't want you in my life… forever. I can't pretend that I don't care what you think about me. I know what I want to hear you say. And yet I have no intention of forcing you to say it."

Belinda remained stoic, chin up, still a little teary-eyed, but determined to maintain her dignity. Only the telltale chewing on her lip gave a hint of that internal conversation that he himself also endured.

"I don't deserve you."

"That's true." Her small smile wavered.

"You've got so much in the success column of life that I'm the charity case who doesn't need to burden your life."

"Charity case? Burden?" Her eyebrows lowered into a deep frown. "From the first time we talked, really talked, I couldn't get you out of mind. You are an anchor for me. I'm used to being on my own and depending on myself, but dammit, Jesse, you are that pillar of strength that I've begun to rely on."

He lifted her chin and gently wiped away a tear.

"Are you really leaving? Did they convince you that they needed you more than I need you?"

"I love you, Belinda. That's what I've been hiding. And I kept it quiet to keep you from having to deal with it. I don't want it to be an open debt, something that you feel that you owe me. But I also know that I don't regret saying it to you. That's why I'm leaving."

"Like hell you are. You're not getting off the hook so easily, Jesse Santiago." Belinda pulled on his arm until he faced her. She gripped his chin. "Look at me." She pointed at her eyes, as if he needed a guide to her loving gaze.

He continued his protest, "I can't give you what I don't have—peace of mind. All my life, I've done things that made me happy. If I saw it, I went after it. And that pursuit of happiness was at the expense of others. Look at what happened with Diego."

Belinda pressed her fingertips against his mouth. "I understand guilt. I've lived with it for most of my life. But it doesn't have to be. Not really. You have got to forgive yourself. Or that beautiful spirit that I love, the essence of the man whom I admire, will disappear."

He didn't respond. His mind had too many thoughts colliding with each other and fracturing.

"You have to make that intention to forgive. As difficult as it has been for you, this burden that you carry is self-made. According to your plan, you don't deserve to be happy." She raised her hand, halting his objection. "You can't love or be loved because it messes with this plan of action."

"Sacrifices have to be—"

Belinda dropped her hands to her sides. Taking a deep breath, she said, "I'm going to walk away. I won't turn back. I won't beg for you to reconsider. I won't sit and brood about the what-if. Because I'm here, in your face, real as ever, telling you that I want you at my side. We make a good team, sweetheart." She smiled on that thought, but sobered quickly. "If you can't admit to loving me and all that it comes with, then I will learn to live with the fact that my intuition is flawed. That all the moments we shared— all our vulnerabilities, my failures, your wins, or your missed opportunities, my accomplishments—have meant nothing, but are just a fond memory for when you and I settle down with other partners." The idea of Jesse with another woman, kids, the dog, a family home to contain their unit…well, it sucked. She had to close her eyes and squeeze them shut to shoo away the image of her handsome lover and his faceless family.

"Woman, you play hardball. I can't let you go." He lifted her chin. Gently, he embraced her face with his hands, cupping either side. "But I'm more in love with you at this very minute than I ever thought I could be last week or the week before that. I love the fight in you. You're my strong woman."

"I will always be that woman for you. And I know when my legs buckle, when I'm exhausted and unsure, your shoulder will be there for me to rest my weary head."

"We are made for each other."

"Yes," she answered.

"How did I manage to fall in love with such a hardhead? I've been trying to tell you for the last five minutes that I love you. Love every part of you. So shut up. Kiss me, my love."

She pressed up onto her tiptoes and fastened her mouth against Jesse's.

Once their lips connected, she knew that she wouldn't and couldn't let go. Magic erupted from their union, spinning out into bands of passion that wrapped them in its cocoon. Snug against his hard body, her body melted and sealed to the muscular plane of his chest and abs and yielded to the pressure of his hard arousal. Any plan to retreat never entered her mind. She didn't have to go there, not when his strong arms encircled her willing body, locking her against him.

"Baby," he groaned against her lips. "You're messing with my head." His tortured moans thrilled her to the bone.

"Still talking…" She shut him up again, kissing him harder, sucking his tongue into her mouth. Without any reservations, she welcomed him like a lover returning from a long trip. Her senses had missed everything about him—the masculine scent of his aftershave, the hungry look that he'd bathed her body with, the sexy dance of his mouth and tongue, the strong fingers that spanned her back and pinned her close. Every fiber of his being she claimed, just as she gave every ounce of herself to him.

She pulled away to catch her breath, just enough not to pass out. His handsome mouth, full and divinely crafted, should not be free for long.

"Should I go tell them the news?" Jesse kissed her forehead.

Olivier and Arthur had walked farther away toward the event that was winding down. They had walked away from the fight.

"Nah. I think they know the answer by now." This was her man, her soul mate, whom she claimed with all the love within her. She'd kept everything in, afraid to share, afraid to open her heart. Together they had muddled through dealing with their own demons to find peace and reach for love.

Her heart was strong. Her spirit was strong. But it had never been put through the test of love. True love, beyond lust and pleasurable sex. Best friends, beyond sharing secrets and innocent hugs. Soul mates, beyond pinky swears of loyalty. No, her heart had never had to stay the course, or sprint along the mad rush of the romantic road as if her life and sanity depended on it.

But she was a granddaughter of the Meadows matriarch. If Belinda had learned anything, she'd taken her lessons directly from her grandmother. No rule existed that a woman shouldn't take the lead to harness her future, even if it meant hitting her man with cold, hard reality—she was worth every thought, action and emotion he had in his life.

"Belinda, I love you, heart and soul, and everything in between."

"And I love you, my handsome man. Every inch, down to a smidgen." She grinned.

"Are you done here? Then let's go seal the deal." His sexy wink delivered its erotic message.

Tawny again stepped into their path. "Not that either of you are aware of the outside world, but I'll volunteer to wrap things up for you while you do… whatever you're going to do." And just as abruptly, she headed off, leaving them to each other's attention.

Belinda's feet were swept from under her as she was cradled against Jesse's chest. Her arms were wrapped around his neck, while she admired the inner glow of his joy that illuminated his entire face. The dark, brooding veil that weighed him down with guilt had slipped off and retreated. They would be all right. That she knew for sure. Her forehead rested against his chin. Comforted with her thoughts, she looked forward to the next few minutes when they'd be together in her bed.

More than ever, she looked forward to the next chapter of their lives intertwined in love and romance.

* * * * *

They're turning
up the heat!

BET ON
My
HEART

J.M. Jeffries

Donovan Russell is trading his five-star Parisian kitchen for the restaurants at his grandmother's Reno casino. Now he just needs his new pastry chef to follow his rules! Because where Donovan is all structure and precision, Hendrix Beausolies cooks with instinct and experimentation. But when someone starts sabotaging their kitchens, they may discover a shared passion for more than just food…

PASSION'S GAMBLE

"Readers get to see the natural and believable progression of a relationship from colleagues to friends to lovers…the journey is a good one." —RT Book Reviews on LOVE TAKES ALL

Available April 2015!

www.Harlequin.com

KPJMJ3980415

A passion for
all seasons…

An Island Affair

**MONICA
RICHARDSON**

Jasmine Talbot is determined to transform her family's Caribbean
property into a one-of-a-kind B and B. But she needs Jackson Conner's
help. A brilliant visionary, the hunky contractor is proud, egotistical…
and impossible to resist. And so is Jackson's powerful desire for his
alluring new boss. But will the secret he's keeping jeopardize Jackson's
budding romance with the dazzling Bahamian beauty?

THE TALBOTS OF ⚓ HARBOUR ISLAND

"[Richardson] writes wonderfully about the difficulties that result when
one's dreams come into conflict with friends and family."
—*RT Book Reviews* on *AMBITIOUS*

Available April 2015!

HARLEQUIN®
www.Harlequin.com

KPMR3970415

REQUEST YOUR FREE BOOKS!

2 FREE NOVELS
PLUS 2 FREE GIFTS!

KIMANI™
ROMANCE

Love's ultimate destination!

The first two stories in the *Love in the Limelight* series, where four unstoppable women find fame, fortune and ultimately… true love.

LOVE IN THE LIMELIGHT

New York Times bestselling author

BRENDA JACKSON

&

A.C. ARTHUR

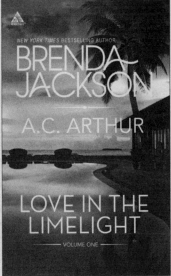

In *Star of His Heart*, Ethan Chambers is Hollywood's most eligible bachelor. But when he meets his costar Rachel Wellesley, he suddenly finds himself thinking twice about staying single.

In *Sing Your Pleasure*, Charlene Quinn has just landed a major contract with L.A.'s hottest record label, working with none other than Akil Hutton. Despite his gruff attitude, she finds herself powerfully attracted to the driven music producer.

Available now wherever books are sold!

HARLEQUIN®
www.Harlequin.com

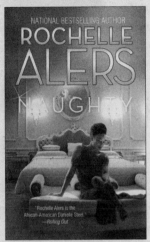

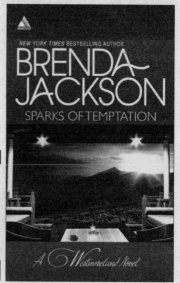